Anonymous

Jonathan Swift

Vol. 2

Anonymous

Jonathan Swift
Vol. 2

ISBN/EAN: 9783337048143

Printed in Europe, USA, Canada, Australia, Japan

Cover: Foto ©Andreas Hilbeck / pixelio.de

More available books at **www.hansebooks.com**

JONATHAN SWIFT

A NOVEL

IN THREE VOLUMES.

VOL. II.

LONDON:

HURST AND BLACKETT, PUBLISHERS,

13, GREAT MARLBOROUGH STREET.

1884.

JONATHAN SWIFT.

CHAPTER I.

VARIOUS feelings of disgust and joy agita-
ted several breasts in Merton when Lauriel accepted the invitation to place herself
at the head of the band of village beauties
who were to do honour to the king; for
of course at Merton on this occasion, as
everywhere else on every other occasion,
no one thought nearly as much about the
ceremony as about the figure he should
cut in it. Lauriel's sweet-tempered affa-
bility prevented, however, any difficulty

on the score of her pre-eminence, and after one or two performances, which Prior, as village master of ceremonies, called dress rehearsals, had helped to make time fly even faster than he is wont, the evening before the royal visit was happily reached.

The only hitch, indeed, had been a very justifiable one, a news-letter had stated that some unknown town in Oxfordshire, called Burford, was going to present the king with two saddles of home manufacture, and the Merton people at once became convinced that the idea was borrowed from *their* proposed libation. This irritated them so highly that they seriously considered abandoning the scheme, until Prior pointed out that, after all, the Burford presentation would be made after the Merton one, and could not therefore detract from their characters as men of original genius. So, after a little grumbling, things were let well alone.

Matthew Prior, in the pseudo-official position I have mentioned, saw a good deal of Lauriel during the three days' interval which elapsed between her acceptance of the proffered honour and the royal visit, and the more he saw of her the more desperately in, what he thought was, love did the poor poet fall. As a natural consequence, he became hourly more anxious to find out who was the mysterious rival he had seen at the cottage. Of course he could have found out by asking the question if there were no secret, and by giving a hint to his guest the 'sergeant' if there were. He had been afraid to do either the one or the other, because he felt that the man was, in fact, this De Guiscard whom the 'sergeant' was making inquiries about, and that Mrs. Swift was criminally responsible for harbouring, and would suffer if detected. By the evening in question, however, a change had come over his love dream. He had been fairly conquered for the first and last time in his life, and had learned to love a woman simply and solely for her own sake without a thought of self.

There is no true love where there is not the spirit of self-sacrifice, of self-abnegation, of self-forgetfulness; but Prior had never known it before, and it came to him as the revelation of a moment. It dawned upon him that the stranger at the cottage was more than his rival, he was the lover of the girl *he* loved. There was not only the question as to whether Lauriel would marry him, but also whether if she married this supposed Monsieur de Guiscard she would be happy. The idea was a new motive power in Matthew Prior's life. The instant it occurred to him he sought his guest, the officer, who was spinning out a useless quest very contentedly, seeing the quarters were good and the fare excellent.

'Well, Mr. Prior,' cried that worthy, as Matthew came in, 'I only want company to make me as happy as a long drink. This liquor is first rate, and the tobacco couldn't be better.' Saying which the jovial officer pledged the whig government at its own expense.

'Then we are agreed,' answered Prior. 'I came on purpose to have a chat; my work is nearly over now—until to-morrow. By the way, how is yours getting on? Is your prey in the neighbourhood?'

'No, thank goodness, I don't think it is. But, of course, I can't be certain on account of having to keep the thing so dark. If I could ask questions of everybody, and put up placards, and offer rewards, I could catch him pretty well, whether he's here or not. As it is, it's different, very different. You have not mentioned the matter to anybody, have you? Ah, that's well. You see my orders were strict to keep my eyes open and my mouth shut.'

'Why, how did they expect you to drink the king's health, then?' said Prior. 'Come, "His Majesty." We are quite alone, I shall be as silent as the grave, tell me something about this highway robber, spy, miscreant, or whatever he may be, 'twill serve to pass away the time and will hurt nobody. To begin with, how long has he been here, if he be here?'

'Well, it can't do any harm to let you know,' replied the other, 'you know how to hold your tongue as well as I do. Let me see now, the fellow was seen here fully a month ago—nearer two, I think.'

Prior began to wonder why in the name of all that was marvellous Mrs. Swift should burden herself with a French spy for a month. Her straitened circum- stances were no secret. Pringle had, with a delicacy which did him infinite honour, hinted at the fact to Prior, for fear too

expensive **ribbons,** &c., **should be** chosen
for Lauriel's dress.

'The girl,' thought Matthew, 'could **not**
have loved him when he first went, even
if she **do now.**'

Then **it** occurred **to** him, are they
bribed? It certainly **looked** very like it.
But then the scene **by the** Devil's Hole
recurred to **him.** Yes, she *did* love him
now; however he might at first have gained
admittance, he was there **now** on the footing of an accepted lover.

'Well,' he said, as these thoughts flashed
through his mind more quickly than I **can**
express **them,** 'now begin with his **cradle,**
and go straight ahead to his gallows.'

'I can't do that, for I didn't trouble to
ask, but **I** believe that, politics apart, the
fellow is a rare blackguard. Fancy a man
being **too bad** for the French army! They
kicked **him** out of that. And fancy a **man**
being too bad to be **an** abbot!'

Prior started to his feet.

'Good God! is the fellow a monk?'

'Ah, I thought that would fetch you,' replied the 'sergeant,' who attributed his friend's agitation to the graphic abruptness of the story. 'Yes, I know that for certain, because the—what do you call the fellows? not Franciscans or Dominicans, never mind, some other "can" (you see, they are all the same as to the "can" tied to their tails, and there's precious little difference in the dogs)—well, I say the lot he belonged to are branded with a cross on their arm when they are sworn in, and I was specially instructed to look for it before I arrested anybody. There's no doubt he was too bad for an abbot; they kicked him even out of that.'

A loud call outside, and a clatter of horses' feet, afforded Prior an excuse to withdraw, which he gratefully seized. His mind was made up. He would warn Mrs.

Swift of his suspicions, let come of it what might. Very possibly, by playing the raven, he would destroy any hope there might be of his ever winning Lauriel's affections; but he had risen superior to that, and, though he saw the danger, he despised it.

Hastily dispatching such duties as bare civility demanded for the comfort of his new guests, and regardless that in all probability the 'Cricket' would be full to overflowing in an hour or two, he started off to Mrs. Swift's cottage, informing his lieutenant where he was going, and alleging as motive some details in to-morrow's ceremony which he had forgotten to explain to Lauriel.

Prior walked slowly, on the whole, though an occasional acceleration of speed, quickly retarded again, betrayed the agitation of his mind. Presently he heard steps behind him, and a contented voice humming a merry tune, and turning round, found Mr. Pringle close behind him, with satisfaction on his face and a parcel in his hand.

'Well,' cried the worthy butcher, 'you look miserable enough in all conscience, and I don't wonder at it. Who told you?'

Prior was shrewd enough to say, 'Oh, I heard,' while inwardly he wondered what was coming.

'Oh,' said Pringle, 'to think she should pick me out of the whole village to do her a good turn! There must be something in it, though heaven knows what she can see in me, and '—a little maliciously—'I can't write poetry.'

'So you are going to the cottage with the parcel?' said Prior, making a random shot.

'Yes,' returned Pringle, 'look. Is this what she wanted, I wonder. I said I would take it to her to-morrow morning, but since I got back to-night she may as well have it now, God bless her.'

So saying, he displayed a yard or so of broad white ribband.

'Where did you get it?' demanded Prior.

'At Nottingham.'

'What? That ribband means a walk of thirty odd miles?'

'Thereabouts.'

Prior looked at Pringle's stalwart frame and then at his honest, beaming face.

'Lauriel Swift might marry a great many people a great deal worse than you,' he said. 'I should be a great deal happier just now if I thought she *was* going to marry you. Are you quite sure you love the girl very much?'

Pringle simply looked at his companion, but it was quite enough. The fund of manly honesty in his clear blue eyes there was no mistaking. So Prior went on.

'Sit down a minute, I have something to tell you;' and forthwith told the great fear that his heart was burdened with.

'You see,' he concluded at last, 'he *cannot* have married her, and he never can marry her, yet I saw him kiss her forehead, and I think I saw the cross on his arm.'

'And you have known this for three days?'

'No,' answered Prior. 'The most important point I only learnt to-night, still I might have found out all earlier had I made an effort. It was very wrong not to do so. Come, let us make an end of suspense.'

Then, without a word more, these two, so unlike in every way but their common love, set gloomily out upon their errand. Just short of the cottage garden, Pringle turned and said, huskily, to his companion,

'Somehow I think you are a born gentleman. I am not. She would understand you better than me. Tell me, will you marry her *at any rate?*' Prior shook his head. 'Then,' said Pringle, drawing himself up, and solemnly uncovering his head, ' I will, so help me, God.'

A few steps more and they stood opposite the great gap, which the falling tree had made in the hedge round Lauriel's garden. The night had clouded over, and it was very dark, so through the gap they could clearly see what was going on in the little cottage parlour, although it was only lit by the flame of a single candle. The window was open too, for De Guiscard's immunity had naturally bred a certain carelessness and feeling of security in his hosts. ' No one will see in but the glowworms,' De Guiscard had urged, and the others readily agreed with him.

Mrs. Swift, Lauriel, and Monsieur de Guiscard were seated round the table admiring the flagon which was to-morrow to be the king's, and which Lauriel had begged leave to take home (at the count's instigation), ostensibly for the sake of practising her part. Prior and his friend had scarcely stood a moment watching, however, before the two ladies rose to go, and that instant De Guiscard walked to the window and shut the shutters. Something in his manner impressed Prior strangely.

'I am going to watch him; come,' he said; and, walking on the trunk, which still lay where it had fallen, through the hedge, he noiselessly made his way, followed by Pringle, over the grass-plot to the window. The woodwork was not of the best, and afforded plenty of chinks through which they could see what followed. Monsieur de Guiscard was standing, deadly pale, listening intently, and then, satisfied the ladies were in fact upstairs he **placed a chair against the door** so as to prevent its **being** suddenly opened, and, drawing a tiny case from **his** pocket, proceeded hurriedly to unfasten it and take out a small brush and bottle. **Then he** paused **and listened** again, **but** all was **still** as death.'

' Antoinette,' **Prior heard** him mutter in **French, 'pour toi!' and** stretching across **the** table he picked **up** the flagon and carefully painted the inside with the fluid contained in the bottle. The strong **hand** of the butcher **closed on** Prior's arm with a grasp of unmistakable **meaning** as by a common impulse they both drew back **from** the window.

' **Is** it for *her?'* gasped Pringle.

' No, **for the king !'**

Just then **the sound of the** shutter-bolt being drawn warned **them** to move behind a bush out **of the light** thrown from the window, **and they** had scarcely done so before, through the new-opened lattice, they again saw De Guiscard move away the chair he had placed by the door and seat himself in a careless attitude, book in hand. Only for a moment; the door was almost simultaneously thrown open, and Mrs. Swift entered again with her daughter. Lauriel had changed her dress for the simple white costume she was to wear on the morrow as first and fairest of the Merton maidens.

'Could any dress suit her better?' cried the mother, with a smile of true maternal pride on her careworn face. 'If the king does not grant any petition whatsoever she chooses to present to-morrow I shall not think him a king in taste!'

'I hope,' returned the count, 'he will not offer half his kingdom without being asked. I am afraid Lauriel would take it, would you not?'

'Really, sir,' she laughed, 'do you suppose me so greedy as to want the whole of it! Come, show me how to hand my scroll. Oh! Henri, suppose the king does not see it, or won't take it! But, do you know, I shall not be nervous, I am sure of that. I shall forget all about the king and the people, and only remember—no, you will be conceited if I tell you, so I shall not.'

De Guiscard reverently raised her fingers to his lips. His hand trembled violently. Noticing it, Lauriel looked up at him with inquiring eyes, and said,

'Henri?'

'It is nothing, my love; I am anxious, unmanned, so much hangs on the success of this attempt—your happiness, too, pretty one! God forgive me for that.'

'Come, you must not think of it,' she said; 'see, be you the king and mamma the people, and I will practise.'

Then she took the flagon and began to

experiment, handing it to De Guiscard, at the same moment drawing from her pocket with her left hand the petition and presenting it also.

'She may put it to her lips,' hissed Pringle; 'I am going to prevent it.'

'Take care, take care,' cried Prior, 'you will frighten her; stay—' but he had darted forward, and, as the next best thing to do, Prior ran to the window, while his friend entered by the door, which chanced to stand ajar, and said, in as natural tone as he could, 'Good evening, Miss Swift, excuse my intrusion, I——' and Pringle was in the room—'Ladies, withdraw, I beseech you.'

Lauriel only shrank closer to her mother, and De Guiscard looked uneasily from the door to the window. Mrs. Swift recovered from her astonishment first, and asked,

'What does this mean?'

'This,' replied Pringle, snatching almost

roughly the flagon from Lauriel and filling it with water **from a bottle on the table.** 'This' (handing it to De Guiscard); 'drink it, poisoner, if you dare.'

'Look, Pringle, look,' shouted **Prior,** 'look **at Lauriel, look** at Miss Swift. For God's sake, **let** the ladies leave the **room.'**

'No,' said Lauriel, in **a** strange, **unearth-**ly voice that made even the baffled criminal standing there forget for a moment his own agony in hers. **'No, I** have a right to **be here, he is my** affianced husband. What have you to say against him.'

'**Poor,** poor child!' said Pringle, in **a** tone **of** intense pity, 'poor, poor **child!'** **and** then, turning in passionate **rage on** the count, '**Dog,** you shall hang for this, **you shall hang** ! hang ! hang !'

Lauriel, bloodless as **a** corpse, moved across the room to her lover.

'Henri, tell me, what does it mean?'

He shrank away from her.

'Let me drink it,' she said, trying to take the fatal bowl, but Pringle interposed.

'Poisoned,' he said, 'and, worse, poisoned by a priest. I could forgive him for being a traitor, but never for deceiving you!'

Prior stepped through the low window into the room, seeing well that all concealment was hopeless. Lauriel must know the worst, and he thought he would tell it more gently than the other.

'Miss Swift,' he said, 'this De Guiscard is a very bad man, I am afraid. He is a spy in French pay. Please go now.'

But Lauriel only stood taking no apparent notice, and saying to herself, 'Priest, priest, priest.'

'Yes, and a priest.'

De Guiscard suddenly roused himself.

'I am unarmed,' he said, 'I am in your hands. You both seem very fond of this

young lady. Come, we will make a bargain. Save my life : let me go : I will re-
linquish my pretensions, and, remember,
*so long as I am safe, so long is her reputation
also.'*

A dull haze came over Lauriel's eyes as
she heard the awful sentence, and a mean-
ingless smile illumined her ashy lips. She
turned without a word, and moved mechanically away. A moment, and her mother
followed her ; another moment and a wild
cry told she had not found her. The two
friends, forgetting everything but love,
dashed to the door.

' Follow her, follow her,' cried the mother, from the room where her darling
was not, ' she has gone out—out into the
darkness !'

And they followed this way and that ;
and Prior, fancying he saw a white dress
flicker a moment amid the trees, ran
eagerly, and saw it again—again—again—

but suddenly it was gone for ever. He paused, and listened, and shuddered, for he could hear the pulse, pulse, pulse of the awful waterfall.

CHAPTER II.

'PRINGLE,' said Prior, when after their fruitless search they met again at the cottage, 'we are bound to inform of this or risk our necks. I know nothing of law, but this much I do know, that it is criminal to conceal the plot we have accidentally discovered. Now, we cannot disclose it without risking the vengeance of that fiend on Lauriel's memory, if it be as I think. For my part, therefore, I shall risk my neck.'

'And I too,' sobbed Pringle, who, great sturdy fellow though he was, was crying like a child.

‘ Then we will say she was ill, and walked out, not knowing where she was, and is
lost. Stay with Mrs. Swift while I run
for the doctor and some woman to take
care of her—look, she needs it,’ and he
pointed to her, where she sat, with pale
grey face, her chin resting on her breast,
and her hands hanging inanimate by her
side—and was gone.

CHAPTER III.

PRIOR, having despatched the doctor to
the cottage, and a kind dame who volun-
teered her services, ran, before returning
there himself, to the 'Cricket' to tell his
man that he should probably be out all
night. He might have been mistaken,
and he would search as long as a hope
remained.

At the 'Cricket' he found to his amazement Henry St. John and a friend of his,
a lanky stranger, whom Prior had never
seen, but who was at once introduced as
'a neighbour of yours, though you haven't
yet the mutual benefits of each other's

acquaintance, " Mr. Swift." He has come on a mission to the king from Sir William Temple, which he expected to discharge at Lincoln, but found his majesty travelled too fast for that, so cut across, and will have the good luck to catch him close to his own door. Why, come, Matt, are not you glad to see us ?'

'Very,' said Prior, suppressing his agitation with great difficulty. 'Come, and choose a bottle of wine in proof of it. Excuse me one moment, Mr. Swift.'

Once outside the room, in a few hurried words he gave St. John an outline of the sad story, omitting, however, all reference to De Guiscard by name.

'What must I do ?' he asked.

'Poor thing,' said St. John, 'I am very sorry for her. But, if you are right, we can do no good. Swift at any rate must not be told till to-morrow. He has a chance in the world to distinguish himself which may never occur again. He loved this sister passionately, I know, and he never could get through his duty to-morrow if the least suspicion of what has come—perhaps—is breathed to him. What a mercy he did not go home to-night; it was too late. He proposes to go after the interview to-morrow. Till then we must try to keep it from him.'

So they did, and next day Jonathan executed his commission without a thought of coming misery to lessen the scope of his mind or weaken the power of his eloquence. And when his majesty complimented him, saying,

'Well, Mr. Swift, I never heard the arguments on your side put so strongly before, you are calculated to be a credit to any profession.'

The first thought in Jonathan's mind was 'how glad the mother and Lauriel will be.'

'I am a soldier,' went on the king, 'so that profession comes first with me; may I post you to a captain's commission in the cavalry?'

'I thank your majesty,' Jonathan said, 'but I am going, I hope, to take holy orders, as that I believe is more in accordance with the bent of my mind.'

'Then,' said the king, 'you must not take orders till I can give you a prebend.'

And again the joy in Jonathan's heart was for the pride his mother would feel and the joyful love of his sister. And then—— St. John had walked with him to the cottage, where Prior met them with a new seriousness on his face.

'Your mother is very ill,' he said, 'very ill indeed.'

Jonathan stopped in the middle of a merry laugh, in which he had wondered at St. John for not joining, and a dread fear came over him.

'Why are you here?' he asked, in a whisper, 'what is it? Not—not—*that*.'

It was madness that he thought of, at that moment, not death.

'Yes,' said Prior, reverently, 'dead.'

And then the motherless son went in to the room where the shadow of the dark valley fell—fell across the golden sunshine of his hope and his happiness. In a little while he came back. The thought they dreaded had intruded on his grief.

'My sister,' he said.

And Prior led him into that tiny parlour, sacred to so many memories of sorrows the breaking heart had not, in God's great mercy, been left to bear alone,—sorrows shared, and joys and hopes shared too, with the loved ones gone for ever, and there he told him all. Very gently he told him, but he told all, for he knew the sister's memory would be as sacred in the brother's eyes as in his own—more sacred even than revenge. He had to tell it twice, for Jonathan's aching mind refused to understand at first, but all at once there went up a cry from a heart misery had conquered.

' Take me too, oh God ! '

CHAPTER IV.

WHO shall imagine the thoughts which crowded in upon Jonathan's bleeding heart during the long night's vigil by his mother's deathbed! He had lost more than mother and sister; more than his nearest and dearest; more than all he could count on as sources to him of human sympathy and love. Far more than all these—he had lost his belief in human nature. 'It would be a terrible thing and a devilish to hate, hate, hate,' he had said, a few days before, to St. John, but he had said it because all in his experience had not been hateful. There had been two whom he passionately loved, and two in whom his trust was infinite. And now—they were gone. Well, he could bow to the Providence of God, and he had their memory still. No, not so! It was far worse than this. He had been deceived. A wound had been made in his trust which could never heal. *He* knew nothing of the specious tale of wrong which had gained a harbourage for his sister's fate, and he could never know, could never suspect it. Why should he?

There were more obvious reasons by far. Money, first of all, money. That will account for a great deal—anything, and it naturally occurred to him first. True, he had sacrificed his very soul, and had gone to Moor Park to drudge, amid scorn and contumely, to earn a living for this mother and sister; but it was little he could do, and they would not be content with little. Anything must be better than existing on a few shillings a week. *Anything*, or who would throw a handsome blackguard for a month into the constant society of an only daughter? What mother would do it, but for gold; and, but for gold, what daughter would consent to it? So Jonathan thought, and the thought burned into his soul like fire. It must have been so, all his being kept asserting, or why were they so reticent. Why, but that they were ashamed. Not one word all those weeks, not a hint even of the fact, much less of the danger. Probably it had all been arranged before he left the house. It must have been, in fact, or else how could the fiend incarnate from whom he had parted on the high road that eventful morning, have dared to return to the cottage and have obtained a welcome?

It was a simple question of money, of pounds, shillings, and pence, Jonathan forced himself to think very calmly. This De Guiscard had returned to the cottage, and bought admission directly Jonathan was out of sight, and the mother had consented in spite of warning, in spite of the peril, alas! so obvious now, for 'thus much money.' And this was his mother, his noble-minded, high-souled, almost angelic mother. She had done this! And Lauriel. She had gone. Sometimes, in after-years, he wondered that at this time he cared so little to discover where she had gone. But *then*, that she had gone was enough. Perhaps she was dead. Prior thought so—was sure of it. And why had she rushed from this world into the presence of her Maker, if that was so? Why had she broken her mother's heart and embittered her brother's soul? Priest! Priest! Priest!!

'How dearly she must have loved the aristocratic lodger,' Jonathan muttered, with a savage delight in probing his own wound ; 'how very dearly.' But of Lauriel he could not bear to think, he dare not. And this was Lauriel, his dear little Lauriel, his sister. What wonder, reader, that after the reflections of that night spent by the side of his dead mother, Jonathan Swift never was the same man again ! What wonder that the great belief in the worth and virtue of his species which had done so much to sustain him, had received a vital shake, and that, in the flash, his shattered idols struck on the steel of trial, he should see illuminated a new view of human nature, a view which showed it to be far indeed from something which it would be a terrible thing and a devilish to hate, hate, hate !

Thinking thus more and more bitterly, more and more convincedly, as the hours passed by, Jonathan sat through the long first night of death alone in the dim-lit chamber. So still he sat that St. John, who in a true spirit of friendship had insisted on spending the night at the cottage for fear poor Swift should want a little human sympathy, fancied, as he stood and listened in the passage, that Jonathan must have fallen asleep. He waited, therefore, till pretty late in the morning before he went to the door with the view of rousing his bereaved friend from his merciful slumber. Directly he knocked, however, Jonathan opened the door and stepped out; evidently he had not slept.

'So! You here?' he said, surprised.

'Yes,' said St. John. 'I thought that perhaps I might be of some use to you—save you some trouble. You won't have the heart to attend to business for a day or two. Poor fellow, I am so very sorry for you. I can't tell you how sorry I am.'

'Thank you,' replied Jonathan, quite calmly. 'It is very considerate of you

to profess such an interest in an almost
perfect stranger;' but all the time he said
it he felt as he had never felt before an
utter disbelief in the reality of his friend's
professions.

It was the first fruit of his latest trial.
He was no longer the optimist in motives,
with his kindliness only tempered by a
supreme contempt of the ordinary intelligence of mankind that he had been a few
hours before. That was over, and for
ever. If his mother and Lauriel had been
mean, petty, wicked, everybody must be
so too.

'You have not slept,' went on St. John;
'come, you will break down at this rate—
you must eat something, and then rest a
little while, and, if you will leave matters
to me, I shall consider it a great privilege
to save you the pain of attending to them
yourself.'

'You mean the funeral,' replied Jonathan, with a perfect calmness which astonished his friend. 'Thank you very much, but I will do it myself. Indeed, I shall go to the village and arrange at once. Afterwards, I must write to Sir William Temple, and give him the result of yesterday's interview, so far as it had any. You see, I remember your own teaching (word for word, indeed, for it was very eloquent) of a week ago. Have you forgotten? You said that " dissipation of mind and length of time are the remedies to which the greatest part of mankind trust in their afflictions. But the first of these works a temporary, the second a slow, effect; and both are unworthy of a wise man. Are we to fly from ourselves that we may fly from our misfortunes, and fondly to imagine that the disease is cured because we find means to get some moments of respite from pain? Or shall we expect from Time, the physician of **brutes, a** lingering **and** uncertain deliverance? Shall we wait to be happy till we forget to be miserable, and owe **to** the weakness of our faculties a tranquillity which ought **to be the** effect **of** their strength?"'

'**No, I** remember **well** saying **so** ; but **I** should not have said it had you **been unhappy.** However, **I** am glad **to see** you bear up so wonderfully well. Pardon me, but **I** did not expect **it, and** that is my excuse for the liberty **I took in** remaining here last night as **I** did. **Well,** perhaps you **would prefer to** be alone, so **I** will go. Good-bye.' And, pressing Jonathan's hand warmly, **he** turned away and **set off** again for Merton.

Henry **St.** John **was very much** surprised **and not** a little put **out** by the apparently callous **way in** which, after **a** few hours had elapsed, his friend bore his great **misfortune.** *We* know that Jonathan could talk quietly of the loss of mother and sister, because that great grief had been overpowered by another which not so much wounded his heart as numbed it; but St. John did not, and so he very naturally thought Jonathan's conduct betrayed a lack of the most ordinary feeling. This flaw in the nature he knew to be so great grieved and hurt him all the more on that very account. No one is troubled when a crack develops in an ordinary breakfast-cup. That, too, is very much the same value cracked or whole, but it is otherwise with an artistic vase. So St. John was forced to think, by the time he reached Merton, that his treasure-trove was not nearly so valuable as he had imagined.

Poor Jonathan! fate was preparing a blow for him here too. He, poor fellow, watched his friend pass away among the trees out of sight, and then, after giving

some quiet directions to the woman who
had come from the village as nurse the
day before, which would occupy her and
prevent her watching him, he crept furtively away—there. And there he stood
calm, impassive, as though no suspicion
crossed his brain of anything but water
having ever sunk in that bottomless abyss,
and listening as though it had no rhythm
for him to the pulse, pulse, pulse of the
torrent. In God's mercy it did not occur
to him then to move six inches further
forward. He would have done it if it had.
But it could not; he was too heart-broken
to remember himself at all, even to that
extent. A man whom misery drives to
suicide is unjustified; he is not miserable
enough to merit death, if he be not too
miserable to remember remedies.

Two days later Jonathan buried his
mother in Merton churchyard. There
were few spectators, and only one

mourner. St. John had gone away the day before, fancying, very naturally, from Jonathan's manner that he was not at all anxious for his sympathetic presence. But that was far from being so, and as the grave was slowly closed, and even the remains of his mother was shut away from him, Jonathan thought bitterly indeed of the 'human kindness' which could not spare an hour or two to save him from feeling so utterly alone just at first. And then the revulsion his great trial had brought about in his soul broke out.

'I will keep a dog to remind me of friendship,' he muttered, as he turned from God's-acre and went back to the living world.

At the gate he was met by Pringle, who had been reverently watching the burial of the mother of her whom he had loved so well.

'I hope you will excuse my presumption, sir,' he said ; ' I wished to show my respect for—for—your poor mother, sir, that is why I am here. And somehow I would like to say good-bye to you before I go away, if you will allow me.'

'Go away?' said Jonathan. 'Where?'

A hard-set look came over the sturdy butcher's face.

'Away from Merton, almost anywhere away from Merton. I hate it! Tell me— you are going to be a clergyman, Mr. Swift, are you not?—you know your Bible, is all that true about the Jews and the Philistines?'

'Quite true,' said Jonathan, fairly surprised into a moment's self-forgetfulness by the man's manner—'quite true.'

'Thank you; then I can ask God's blessing on what I am going to do. Perhaps you will know all about it some day. Do it I will, if it take me as long as it took *them* in the wilderness. Good-bye.'

'Good-bye,' said Jonathan.

A moment after Pringle turned back.

'Mr. Swift,' he asked, 'where are *you* going?'

Jonathan paused before he answered. It had never occurred to himself that he must go somewhere, and that the main reason for his life at Moor Park was removed; but it all flashed across him now. And he looked mentally around him on the bleak waste of life where no road appeared brighter than another. Yes, it would be simpler to go back, and no whit more dismal; so he said, after the momentary survey.

'To Moor Park—this afternoon.'

'Thank you; there is something I might have to write to you about, that was all. Good-bye.'

There were years to pass and changes to happen, and Moor Park was to be a memory before that message came.

CHAPTER V.

ALL news travelled slowly in those days, and a very great deal did not travel at all. A shipwreck, murder, or petty larceny is made to feed a great many more intelligences now than in the seventeenth century. In 1695 each village or township successfully consumed its own news, whether good, bad, or indifferent, and had nothing to supplement it but the London letter.

So, of course, Jonathan arrived at Moor Park with his misfortune unheralded as it would have been to-day by the friendly labours of a sensational reporter; and he

had written no word himself beyond the
report of his interview with the king.
Therefore it was that, as Jonathan's post-
chaise drew up at the end of its homeward
journey, Hestor Johnson, standing with a
sunny face on the lawn beyond the carriage
drive, called merrily across,

'Welcome back, Mr. Swift, I have two
surprises for you, and I think Sir William
has another—at least, if the news-letter is
true.'

Jonathan forced a smile, but did not
trust himself to speak. She seemed,
standing there, so bright an embodiment
not only of beauty and of life, but also of
truth and goodness, while Lauriel——

'Oh, God!' murmured the poor riven
heart as, mechanically, Jonathan walked
upstairs to his master's study, 'oh, God!
Why didst Thou not take her sooner while
I could have loved her still?'

'Dear me,' thought Hestor, 'how gloomy

he is. I'm **afraid** the king **has not** been very civil to him, after all; however, this letter will soon cheer him up. How **stupid** of me, perhaps they told **him.** I do hope not. Well, I must wait.'

And while she waited Jonathan was plunging into business with Sir **William.** It was a **relief to** him **to be** forced to think about anything **other** than **his bitter sor-** row, **and** he flung himself into his **work** with a feverish **energy which** puzzled the worthy baronet, who was far too shrewd **a** diplomatist **to** imagine for **a** moment that his secretary really **felt** that interest in the triennial bill which **he appeared to do.**

'Are you ill, Mr. Swift?' he **asked,** presently.

'I? Oh, **no,'** returned Jonathan, 'I feel perfectly well, thank **you,** perfectly. Very possibly **I may** be pale, however. My rest **has** been a great deal **broken** during my absence owing **to—h'm—grief** at the sudden death of my mother—and sister.'

'Dear me, I am exceedingly sorry to hear it. It is very sad when a young person is taken away, especially. Your mother, I suppose, could scarcely have lived many more years in any case.'

'No,' said Jonathan, 'not many. She was not an old woman, by any means, but she had had more trouble than one generally has in a much longer life. It is satisfactory to me now,' he went on, with a scarcely disguised bitterness, 'having lost them so soon, that I did *not* let my sister go out to service and my mother to charing.'

'Yes,' said Sir William, 'it is all very well; but it might not have been so. My advice was perfectly sound as matters then were. However, I am very sorry for you, and if you feel work just now to be irksome, take a holiday for a day or two by all means. I can get on very well for a little while alone. Besides, you have earn‑ed a rest in all fairness, for, partly owing to your representations, his majesty has privately informed several of the leading men on both sides that he will do in this matter as the houses of parliament may desire. You may possibly do very well in the world with care and application if you choose. Are you ambitious?'

'I think I was once. To be the greatest of men really seems as petty an outlook as to be the best of them. For long my ambition was a missionary one; the desire to improve by divine means the lives around me. That seemed the most glaring necessity of the age—of all ages. That seemed the grandest field to work in, the most magnificent as well as the most holy. Now, I am not so sure. Certainly the harvest *is* plenteous, but it is a harvest of weeds and thistles; and it seems to me that raising men in sanctity is like raising criminals on a ladder only to ensure their having a deeper drop in the end.'

'You are too bitter,' said Sir William. 'All ladders are not to gallows. There was one which went up into heaven.'

'Yes,' retorted Jonathan, 'there was *one*, but it was for angels. However—and, as to resting, it is a relief to me to work, especially political work. I am in a political frame of mind.'

'What frame is that?' said Sir William, humouring him.

'Midsummer, the antithesis of Christmas and its song—strife on earth and hatred to my fellow-men. Pray, pardon me for this egotistical conversation; it can have no possible interest for you, nor for myself, for the matter of that. One only loves oneself if one is loved; it is a condition of human nature; so, as my mother and sister were the last earthly friends I had, the only ones who loved me, I have a difficulty in caring sufficiently for myself to inspire a personal pronoun at all.'

'You will see things in a brighter light soon,' replied Sir William; 'do plenty of work and take plenty of exercise. Brace mind and body, and you will soon be juster both to yourself and others. I am off now to call on the new rector (Dr. James's successor, you know).'

'He has come, then?' said Jonathan.

'Yes. Ah, by the way, it is since you went north. Good day, then. I shall probably not see you again until to-morrow.'

So he went, and Jonathan, looking after him with a vague curiosity, observed that he leaned somewhat heavily upon the bannister as he walked downstairs.

'Time is beginning to weigh upon him,' thought our hero, as he presently followed.

' If Death were wise, he would always spare diplomatists ; they cater for him so assiduously and well.'

He had forgotten all about Hestor Johnson, or he would have gone to his room instead of his old haunts in the pleached alleys, till a merry laugh broke in upon his reverie. He looked up with an expression of weary sadness, and she saw he was more than gloomy.

' I beg your pardon, Mr. Swift; I hope I am not disturbing you. This letter came the day you went' (holding it up), ' and it occurred to me you might like to read it.'

Jonathan caught a glimpse of the writing and knew it instantly : it was Lauriel's. Before he could speak, she went on—

' You are not ill, I hope ? It is true you succeeded very well with the king, isn't it ?'

With the letter in her hand, of a date

so recent, a letter full of life and joy, clear as the carol of a lark, hopeful as spring, to ask, 'Is Lauriel well?—is your mother well?' never crossed her imagination. As for him, he said nothing. He burned with anxiety to read the letter. There might be some hint in it, some forecast, some clue to what was coming, oh, so soon after it was penned. And he had a dim dread that, if she knew, Hestor might think it best he should not see it.

'I will read it to you,' she went on, 'carefully omitting the compliments, for fear they should make you conceited, although I suppose you know that a sister's opinion invariably *is* more favourable behind a brother's back than to his face. I daresay she bullies you and makes fun of you endlessly enough when you are at home. Know ye that these presents are from Lauriel Swift to Hestor Johnson, as follows.' And then she read, while Jonathan sat on a garden seat, sheltering his face from her view by resting his forehead on his hand.

'"Dear Miss Johnson,

'"Pray excuse my writing to you, but perhaps, under the circumstances, you will not think it odd I should do so. My brother Jonathan, who is Sir William Temple's secretary just now, is my only brother, and I am his only sister, yet, in spite of this, the bad boy either won't or can't write me so much as one letter per annum worthy of the name. That is to say, beyond the implied information that he is in the land of the living, there is no suspicion of news in his epistles—never, not once. What he does, where he goes, and how his world wags generally—in short, just whatever his mother and I like to hear about is precisely what he never mentions. Now from his letters, in defiance of the above facts, I have gleaned one scrap of information, namely——" I shall miss that out.'

'Please don't,' said Jonathan; 'I want to hear every word of it.'

'On no consideration,' she laughed. 'You have been libelling me, and your sister is quoting it, that is all. Well, to proceed:

'"So blame him if I am wrong. But I don't believe for a moment I am, so I have no hesitation in trespassing on your good nature to the extent of asking you to let me hear occasionally of what is going on at Moor Park. I am sorry you have nobody here you care about, or I could reciprocate. Merton news would not interest you, even if there were any—which mercifully there is not. The best I could tell you would be the latest trick of my pet jackdaw—you see the blot, the little wretch stole my pen this minute—or that the

village hotel is under entirely new management. It is all so different when there
is somebody you love. It makes me as
happy as a lark to write to you about
him. You don't know how we love him.
He is the dearest brother alive, and the
cleverest too. He will be great some day,
you know: yes, I'm sure you know. Nobody could talk to him for long without
finding that out. It will come all in good
time. And when it does come it will be
the best thing in the world for everybody.
You will laugh at my enthusiasm, I daresay. Well, though I know I am right, I
should not have written so hopefully most
days in the week. But to-day is what we
call a Jonathan day, that is to say, one so
bright and beautiful that Jonathan won't
do any work, saying it is a natural holiday
and to work on it is wicked. If he were
here we should go in the woods and lunch
off bread and apples, as orthodox picnic

fare, and laugh and chatter nonsense. I wish we could go to-day, and that you were coming too. Some day perhaps we shall. Now, good-bye, and if any time you have nothing to do and will write me a word of news about my bad brother, you don't know how much obliged I shall be to you.'"

'There! What shall I write back?'

'My poor sister will never get the answer, Miss Johnson.'

Hestor looked in amazement, and understood now the far-off look in his eyes.

'I am so sorry,' she said, her eyes filling fast with tears. Her voice soothed him as nothing else had done yet. 'Forgive me for paining you so.'

'I wished to hear it,' said Jonathan. 'There might have been something in it to make the blow easier to bear. It was the last letter, the last hope, a voice from the grave. But there is nothing. I—' but his voice failed him, and, turning abruptly, he went away.

Certainly the letter had made his trouble, if that were possible, more heavy. He knew that Lauriel, when she wrote that letter, was looking forward with delighted expectation to the royal visit and the part in it she was to play. He knew that Henri de Guiscard was under the same roof with her when she wrote it, possibly at her elbow, yet the letter was silent, though the heart was full.

'I am bound,' he thought, as he went to his room and shut himself away from intrusion, 'I am bound as much to follow the dictates of reason in this case as I would in another where I felt not at all. Mother and Lauriel have gone to their graves with a secret beyond all question. What it was I shall never know here.

Please **God** it **may be** one **they** shall **not** be ashamed to tell me in the world hereafter.'

CHAPTER VI.

' ALL philosophy agrees that the consideration of the infinite is the most effective sedative for sorrow.'

I forget who says so and I really cannot say it of my own knowledge. Indeed, I am strongly of opinion that it is not true, and that all philosophy never does agree about anything. That is unnatural philosophy. The unanimity of *natural* philosophers shows what a miserable lot of mathematicians they are! However, Hestor Johnson's idea was the old-fashioned one that the way to be happy was to make others happy, and she frequently thought of the maxim in connection with our hero. For day after day, week after week, passed away and saw Jonathan going listlessly through a round of set duties to which he was perfectly indifferent.

Talking to no one when he could avoid it, and not even reading to while away the tedious monotony of time and thought, his life was a bare existence, and his being seemed to have no object. Hestor, of course, did not fully understand it. She had no knowledge of anything beyond the bare loss he had sustained; but that the great soul, overflowing with passionate earnestness to benefit his fellow-creatures, had received a rude shock which made it doubt for a moment whether there were such things as virtue, and goodness, and truth; she could not tell, and never suspected. Indeed, at this time (and not till long afterwards) she was not at all fully aware of this the leading feature of Jonathan Swift's character. Few but the mother and sister he had lost guessed how much he was animated by the spirit of a better Loyola, or recognised the compatibility of his gibes, sometimes bitter, sometimes playful, at the stupidity of his species with the love he bore the beings created—at least, as to their moral nature—in God's own image. It was not a subject about which he cared to talk, unless when warmed to it by the grating sentiments of some of those puppies who were as common then as now, though perhaps not quite so blatant, and who judged of others' virtue by their own. And, in his actions, with a conscientiousness which it is very easy in such cases to overdo and which, in spite of the sneers generally levelled at subscription lists and the like, I believe, is as often overdone as not, he took the utmost care that his right hand and his left were never, if he could help it, ac-

quainted with what each other did. So
even had Hestor guessed from the silence
he preserved on the subject of his sister's
death that there was something he wished
to hide, something more than a mere be-
reavement over which he sorrowed, still
she could not have told what a wrench had
been given to the whole of that great
nature. She knew enough, however, and
saw enough to make her young heart very
sad for Jonathan's sorrow. With feminine
tact she used to contrive all sorts of means
by which he was forced for courtesy's sake
into a few minutes' conversation or into
doing something that, in a sense, at least,
diverted him; but all in vain. The weeks
passed swiftly away, but the jaded, listless
face looked more jaded and listless than
ever.

Hestor determined that she would make
a crowning effort.

'Mr. Swift,' she said one day, 'I want

to talk to you a little while, if you can spare a few minutes.'

'Certainly,' replied Jonathan, smiling faintly, 'I shall be very pleased.'

So they sat down, and she rushed straight into the heart of her subject, being a good deal alarmed at her own temerity.

'Mr. Swift, I think you are very wicked!'

'Why?' asked Jonathan, fairly startled into attention.

'Yes, very wicked,' she went on, 'and I'll tell you why. You think only of yourself, you think only of how miserable you are—oh! I am so sorry—but you have no right to. That is not what you were sent into the world for. You are clever, you know it, just as well as I do. Were those abilities given you simply to understand your miseries the better and appreciate them more keenly? Was your powerful memory conferred simply to enable you **to** intensify your grief, to facilitate the recall-**ing** of every trait which could add bitter-ness to sorrow and poignancy to anguish? Or was **that** best gift of a powerful Crea-tor, a boundless imagination, made yours that **trials** should become unbearable through **the** constant picturing of **a** roseate happiness that might have been? No, **Mr.** Swift, you are wrong, and you know it. You ought to bear **your** wounds bravely, and work manfully in spite of them with **all** your **energies** and talents for the good of your fellow-men and—it should not sound like cant to **say** it to one who proposes to pursue **the** career of a clergyman—for the glory **of** God.'

Jonathan looked at the fair young face, radiant with **the** timid consciousness of doing a right superior to etiquette, and was puzzled how to reply.

'Is it possible,' he said, evasively, 'to benefit mankind?'

'I don't know,' returned Hestor, boldly, 'but I know it is right to try, and I know it is wicked not to. We have no right to believe as you and I believe, and in the same breath to declare that human nature is incapable of amendment and human life of melioration; and at any rate we know that every effort faithfully made for others, be its effect what it may on them, is beyond all doubt and question a blessing to ourselves.'

'But it very much depends on one's self whether such efforts are possible. For me it would be a primary impossibility to embark on an enterprise which I felt was assured of failure. Miss Johnson, I have thought as you think, but it was before I realized, not so much the magnitude, as the infinity of the task. It was my ambi-

tion to devote my life in its entirety to the
relief from suffering and rescuing from sin
of the miserable and the degraded; it was
my daily prayer that I might be an instru-
ment in the hands of Divine goodness for
the raising of the fallen and the cheering
of the faint and heavy-laden; it was my
all-absorbing anxiety to promote the coming of that Kingdom in which the tears
shall be wiped away from off all faces and
the stains from off all hearts. But I did
not see then as I see now, nor understand
my fellows then as I understand them
now, nor recognize the impossibility of the
task I set myself.'

'It was a grand ambition,' she said,
standing in her youth and beauty like a
prophetess of old, ' and it shall be grandly
fulfilled. One way or another it is sure to
be; an ambition always is. And you will
fulfil yours. Perhaps not exactly as you

think or wish, but it will be fulfilled somehow. An ambition to do right is a prediction that one will do it.'

He was warmed by her enthusiasm, in spite of himself.

'Fortunately there is little to be done in our immediate neighbourhood,' he said; 'there is little sin and suffering, because'—and the gradually prevailing feeling broke through—'there are few people.'

She saw her point was carried, nevertheless.

'No,' she said, 'but there is always room to do good, even among the best and happiest of mortals; and besides, I don't think you know how much distress there is just now, even in the ordinarily happy villages around us. Fever and famine have been at work almost unimpeded. The assistance Sir William and those like him have given has been given indiscriminately and, as a consequence, with very little effect, and, while the poor cottars have had but misdirected charity afforded them, of sympathy and solace they have had absolutely none.'

'Has the new rector done nothing?' asked Jonathan, with a newly-awakened interest that gladdened Hestor's heart.

'Very little,' she said. 'He goes now and then, and he is generous too. But he does not *feel* for the poor, and they know it. Say, will you promise me you will go and do what you can to help? Please do.'

'Since you ask me—yes, I will,' replied Jonathan. 'It is very kind and good of you to trouble about me at all. Yes, I will go.'

And, as good as his word, the same afternoon he trudged off to Woolham, that being the hamlet in which he expected the proportion of distress, moral, mental, physical, and spiritual, would probably be greatest. He was a little angry with himself for having surrendered so readily to Hestor's entreaties.

'I shall do no good,' he kept repeating inwardly, as he walked along, 'no real good. Can I make them better than Lauriel, or happier? And yet certainly I shall inflict a great deal of suffering on myself.'

For suffering it very really was to him to go back into the world. It was not a very hopeful spirit in which to embark on a missionary enterprise. Presently he met a horseman who stopped as he approached him, and asked politely what was the large building in the distance of which they could see the towers.

'I don't know,' said Jonathan; 'probably either a prison or an hospital. Anything large of human contrivance is sure to refer to either the follies, crimes, or sufferings of men. Their virtues and felicity are not so cumbersome. Good morning.'

The horseman looked curiously after him as he strode away. Jonathan caught his look as he turned.

'He thinks I said that for the sake of the wit, if there were any,' he thought. 'It would surprise him to know I really meant it—and believed it!' Then he stopped short and asked himself, 'Is there any rational ground for supposing that a man actuated by such a spirit as gave utterance to that sentiment can do any good to anybody, or even really sympathise with others?'

The days were coming when a bitter sneer at his species would be meat and drink to Jonathan Swift; but those were not yet. He felt a little ashamed of himself, and turned aside into a pretty plantation bordering on the road, to think whether he should go on or not. The spot was one peculiarly calculated to inspire the mind with those kindly feelings towards others which so largely spring from being exceedingly comfortable oneself. The tufted ground sloped down to a swift-flowing mill-stream, and through the feathery green of the young pine-trees one could see a corner of the mill wheel, and away beyond it that most picturesque of objects, a plain luxuriant with furze.

Jonathan sat down, and was about to commence his introspection, when he caught sight of a ragged urchin, who, rod in hand, was furtively creeping along the stream in search of some convenient spot from which to rob the miller of his fish. He looked hungry, not to say half-starved, and had much more the air of fishing for life than recreation. Jonathan sat still and watched him try several unsuccessful casts. The trees were in the little fellow's way, and to avoid them he crept more and more near to the edge. In spite of his efforts, however, the line presently became entangled with a bough in a position quite out of his reach, and, after a few desperate attempts to release it, the tired little body flung itself despondingly down, and the sunken little eyes filled with tears.

Jonathan rose and walked towards him, intending to set his tackle free, and quite oblivious of the poaching aspect of the question. The boy was not, however. In his sobbing he did not hear Jonathan's approach until within a few feet of him, but then, starting to his feet with a cry of fright, he turned and fled. He had forgotten how close he was to the water's edge, and before he could recover himself had fallen with a splash into the swift-flowing current, and was swept down with it towards the mill. Regardless of the danger, Jonathan instantly leaped in after him, and swam vigorously to the drowning boy. Five minutes of desperate work, and then a painful fear they had been in vain, as the ragged figure lay motionless on the bank, the face deadly pale and the eyes half-closed. At length signs of life answered Jonathan's efforts, and directly he was sure breathing was re-established he wrapped the scarcely animate speck of mortality in his own coat, which he had pulled off before jumping into the water, took him in his arms, and, getting back to the road, ran with him as fast as he could to Woolham. The warmth of his body, heated with running, had restored the poor little fellow to some glimmering consciousness by the time the village was reached.

'I'm very—sorry—mother—I couldn't catch any fish—I'm afraid you're very hungry—mother.'

Then silence again.

'Where does this boy live? Does he

live here at **all?'** **asked** Jonathan of the first labourer he met.

The man directed him, but it was some minutes before Jonathan discovered where it was he meant, nothing in his previous experience, varied as that had been, having prepared him to look for the abodes of human beings in hovels not nearly as **proportionately** commodious as is its hole to **a rat.**

' Let me walk,' murmured the boy, coming to himself for **a** moment, ' mother will be frightened.'

There **was no need for our** hero **to** remonstrate, for the little fellow's strength ebbed again and he fainted **away.** **There was** no one in the hut (to dignify it **with that** name) just then, and **Jonathan** looked round in amazement **at** the abject poverty it disclosed. There was no furniture whatever but **a** broken chair, a box **turned** upside down, and a kettle.

I have seen places like that myself, and
I have seen the people who live in them.
I daresay you all have : and I was sorry,
as I daresay you all were, and lamented
the grinding poverty which made neces-
saries luxuries and comforts incredible;
and I have been cut to the heart by the
crime which fed on the poverty, and the
demon that promised forgetfulness only
to make it more necessary to forget; and
I have thrown with a sigh a sixpence, or a
shilling, or a sovereign into that ocean of
grief and woe unspeakable, and then gone
home and dressed for a dinner at which
every extravagance combined to defeat
the bounty of Nature, and neutralise the
loving-kindness of the Creator of the sea-
sons. It is the universality of such conduct which saves it from being characterized as it deserves. It will be some day;
but meanwhile we call it 'Loving one's
neighbour as oneself.'

Jonathan laid his burden in a corner and went at the top of his speed to borrow some blankets, and to get a little wine or spirit wherewith to reanimate him. When he got back the mother was bending over her boy, chafing his hands with breathless anxiety, and wringing the water from his hair.

'It's mother, Jimmy, it's mother; open your eyes, Jimmy, open your eyes,' she wailed. 'He is not—not going, is he? My boy, my Jimmy. Bring him back, for God's sake, bring him back to me.'

'Never fear,' said Jonathan, cheerfully, —it was the first semblance of cheerfulness he had assumed since that day at Merton—pouring some brandy down the unaccustomed throat, 'we shall pull him round famously. Help me to get off his wet things and wrap him up. See, rub his legs well with the brandy. There, his eyes are opened; kiss him, it will do him good.'

When they had fairly brought their patient round, Jonathan bethought him of the mother, who seemed but little further from the Great River than her boy had been.   Starved, pinched, shivering with ague, dressed in tatters, there was something nevertheless in her manner and movements that distinguished her from that great majority of mankind who are in the same circumstances.   Jonathan did not trouble about *that*, however, for the moment.   It was sufficient to manage about food and fire ; so, giving some directions which would keep her occupied till his return, he started off again to see what could be done, and before long had a good fire burning and some warm bread and milk ready on the box table.

'Good-bye now,' he said, 'I will call again to-morrow morning, and expect to find the boy much better.   Take care to eat the bread and milk while it is warm, it will do you good.'

And then, **having** been upwards **of two** hours in his wet clothes, and oblivious **of** the fact that he **was chilled to the bone,** he made off **for** Moor Park.

'You **should have** taken some **brandy** yourself,' said Hestor, when she knew. But it had never occurred to him.

CHAPTER VII.

VERY naturally Hestor Johnson was much interested in the story Jonathan told her on his return, and the next day she accompanied him when he went to visit the widow and the fatherless in their affliction. They found Jimmy lying quite still, paler, if that were possible, than ever, watching with lack-lustre eyes, the smoke escaping through the leaky roof.

'See,' said Jonathan, cheerily, 'I have brought you back your line, and Miss Johnson has got some jelly for you and mother. We must get some colour into your cheeks, and have you running about again.'

The little fellow smiled a grateful smile, but seemed too weak to speak.

'You are very kind and good,' said the mother, 'you have saved my boy—all I have left in the world. I will pray for you always.'

To a good many people there would have seemed something irresistibly ridiculous in a person praying for another's good who had apparently got so little by praying for her own; but Jonathan raised his hat, and said, solemnly,

'Thank you, I hope you will, and I daresay you don't guess how much I need it.'

Then they set to work and fed the boy with some jelly moistened in port wine, and he, soothed by the unusual delicacy, soon fell into a comfortable sleep. Every day Jonathan, sometimes alone, but more generally accompanied by Hestor, paid such a visit and found his patient as often worse as better. He began to be seriously alarmed that the worst was only a little deferred, and one day when he found the exhaustion more pronounced than ever, and wondering whether there was nothing which could lighten the shock to the poor mother if it came, he asked her,

'Is Woolham your native place, Mrs. Grey? Have you no friends elsewhere?'

She went and looked at her boy. He was sleeping heavily.

'I will tell you all about it,' she said, coming back, 'I think you will understand. Most people don't see it as I see it. But, whether or not, you will go on being kind to Jimmy, won't you? it isn't his fault; and if I am taken away from him you will look after him a little, perhaps. He is a very good boy, God bless him, and will work, but he is not over strong at his best, and can't do the rough jobs some of them can. And I never knew him tell a lie but once when we were very badly off. I think for two days we had eaten nothing. Well, a farmer gave him a piece of meat-pie, and he brought it home and told me he had given him his dinner as well, so that that was for me. And he sat there and watched me eat it all, every bit, God bless him.'

And the mother stepped quietly across again and softly kissed the pinched, wan face. Hestor, who was there that day, had some ado to keep from crying.

'I found it out,' went on Mrs. Grey, 'when I thanked the farmer. He said my boy would go to hell, which was made for liars, and that not another bite should he have from him.'

'I suppose,' interposed Jonathan, in a tone of unspeakable scorn, 'he is a Scotch-man, and comes from either Glasgow or Inverness.'

'I don't know,' continued Mrs. Grey.

' That was the only time he ever said what wasn't true. But you are not like the farmer, you will understand both me and Jimmy when I tell you all about myself. Shall I ?'

' I should like to know,' said Hestor, ' if it won't pain you to tell, because perhaps Mr. Swift or I may be able to do something for you if we knew.'

So, only breaking-in upon her narrative to go occasionally to see that Jimmy's head was comfortably on the pillow Hestor had given, the wretched mother told the following story :

' My father was an Englishman, but my mother was a Frenchwoman, and, as she preferred the Continent very much to England, we generally lived either in France or Switzerland. When I was about twelve years old my father died, leaving my mother exceedingly well-off, not to say rich, and with only myself and my sister to take care of. An elder brother—the only one I ever had—had died some years before. Our mother, after considering well all the circumstances of her position, at last decided to go and live for the next five or six years at an old chateau which was fortunately to let, and which was so happily situated as to combine the comforts and seclusion of the country with the advantages of town, the university town being just within driving distance. This she did very much to the delight of my sister and myself. We revelled in the woods and shrubberies, we rejoiced in listening to the birds, and fancied we should never tire of the tranquil pleasures such a life afforded.

' Our mother, who was bent upon carrying out what she knew had been our father's wishes towards us, spared no expense on our education, although she personally regarded letters as quite beyond a woman's province excepting only writing, reading, and a little poetry. Masters were procured from the University to teach us all the subjects our father had intended to himself have taught us had he lived, and we very soon acquired a smattering of the dead languages, astronomy, and the like, sufficient to make us pass in the eyes of those more ignorant than ourselves for accomplished ladies. Neither Rita—my sister—nor myself cared for studying, however, and before a couple of summers had passed at the château we were a little tired of the monotony of country life. Our mother nevertheless, was firm. It was best for us, she said, in every way, and she would not consent to more than occasional visits of a week or so at a time to the gaieties of the outside world.

'One day, after a peculiarly dull fortnight, during which the rain had prevented our indulging even in those sub-

stitutes for enjoyments which are called
rural pleasures, we heard that a theatre
was to be temporarily opened in the town.
It was as though we had been told that
Paradise began in the next room. But
the door was locked. Rita asked to be
taken—in vain. Then I asked—in vain.
Then we both went together, and cried
over it. Mamma wavered. I was sixteen then, and no doubt mamma thought
that a girl of sixteen, who could cry over
not going to the play, was not one who
would get much harm by going. So we
went to town for the week, full of the
promise we had extracted that we should
go twice at least to the theatre. Rita and
I during the intervening weeks talked of
nothing, dreamed of nothing, thought of
nothing, but the theatre. But I should
tell you that it was always the theatre in
connection with each other: so it was in
all our pleasures. She loved me more

than life, and I—I cannot tell you how I loved her. We were never apart for an hour at a time without being miserable in consequence. Pleasure without Rita was pain to me, just as pleasure without me was pain to her. We were very much alike, too, in every respect. Our hair, eyes and complexions, were alike, yet there was no mistaking the one for the other. There were some lines and points of expression in each face that effectually distinguished each from the other. I am a good deal changed,' went on Mrs. Grey, with a weary sigh, 'yet my expression is very much, I think, as it used to be, but my sister, my darling Rita, she was more like this——'

Jonathan, remembering the boy asleep in the corner, smothered his rising cry of amazement, and Hestor, warned by his 'hush,' did so too; but it was an effort, and no wonder, for there sat a person bearing no more than a family likeness to Mrs. Grey; the same in some respects and yet altogether different, it would have been impossible to assert the identity of the individual they were looking at with Jimmy's mother. Letting her features resume their ordinary expression, Mrs. Grey went on.

'But perhaps the most distinctive point about us lay in our voices. There was a difference in tone that the most casual listener could scarcely avoid noticing, if he noticed anything at all. I have been speaking in my own voice, Rita's was more like this——'

This time neither Jonathan nor Hestor could suppress a cry of amazement. The voice they heard was not a squeak, nor a falsetto, nor an imitation, it was another voice, as clear, easy, natural as the speaker's own, and yet as perfectly different as day from night.

'Well,' went on Mrs. Grey, 'the time for going to town came round at last, and at length one never-to-be-forgotten evening saw us safely at the theatre. I watched to see who was looking admiringly at Rita, and she no doubt was as interested in my triumph. Presently I noticed a tall, aristocratic-looking man seated opposite to us and observing my sister most admiringly. But just then the play began, and I forgot everything but the joys and sorrows on the stage. That play absorbed my very soul. I had expected to be interested—I was entranced. When the curtain fell, I had quite forgotten where I was; even Rita and mamma had vanished utterly from my mind. When we got home and I was going to bed, I dressed myself like the heroine who had so much attracted my sympathy, and, looking as like her as I could, suddenly turned round to Rita who always shared my room. Poor Rita screamed when she saw me and nearly fainted. I was so changed she did not recognise me, and thought she saw a ghost. Then she tried, but quite unsuccessfully. She could not imitate the actors as could I. It was a natural gift of mine. I am going to tell you the use I put it to.

'Next day the tall, handsome man I had seen at the theatre called upon mamma. She was very displeased when the name was announced, but seemed to think it best to admit him, and, when he came in, I saw who it was. He stayed a long time, and paid a great deal of attention to Rita on the plea of being her cousin; but mamma said afterwards that he was only a remote connection by marriage. However, both we girls thought him charming, whatever he was. He seemed to have been everywhere and seen everything. There was a scar, too, on his face from a sabre cut, that was peculiarly fascinating to us.

Well, he came and came again and again,
even after we had gone home to the
chateau.   Mamma kept us out of the way
as much as she could without forbidding
him the house, and that she was loth to
do to a relation, however remote.   So it
went on for three or four months, during
which the intervals of his visits were spent
by both my sister and myself in looking
forward to the next one and in acting some
such congenial play as "Romeo and Juliet."
Mamma at length (alas! too late) thought
it necessary to interfere.   She wrote a
kind but final note to monsieur requesting
him not to call again, and casually told us
girls she had done so, saying that she had
become aware monsieur was a very bad
man.

'That was not to be the end, however.
Three months later there came a letter
from him to mamma asking for Rita's hand,
and another to Rita saying he had tried to

live without her **and could** not, professing
undying love for her. Mamma would
have told Rita nothing about it, but as **it**
was she could not help doing so. So she
spoke to her as tenderly as only mother
could speak, praying her not to think **of**
this bad man, but to write and send him
away. Rita kissed mamma, but said nothing.
She was not much more than seventeen
years old, and, though **I** was **a full** year
younger, she generally allowed herself to
be led by me, while as for mamma **I** had
never till that day known Rita disobey her
merest wish. It **was not to be so** now.
After vainly trying to obtain mamma's
consent, at last, in desperation at our con-
templated removal to England, my sister
ran away with this man.

'It was one evening she went—I know
all about it now. **He** was to meet her at
eight o'clock in **a glade** near **the** chateau,
and had bribed the curé to marry them at

once. Poor mamma was terribly grieved about it, but she was very angry too. Thinking I must have known something about it, she was very angry with me as well, and I don't think she ever afterwards trusted me as entirely as she had done before. Now I must tell you about the money.

'My father left all his property to my mother, and to us after her death in such proportion as she thought fit, hoping thus to neutralise the consequence of either of us marrying much better than the other. Thus, you see, my mother could, had she chosen, have left all her money to me. Monsieur soon found this out, and provided against it in the only way he could. Of course I did not know it was he then, remember: and remember, too, that I loved him, that I had loved him all along, and could not help loving him, even now he was married to my sister. He was the very last person I ever should have suspected or imagined guilty of the awful deed I am going to tell you of. Oh! God, the agony of knowing who had done it, that agony that came years later, mercifully was greater even than the anguish of learning what was done when it *was* done.'

She paused a moment to recover her self-possession, and then said, solemnly,

'My mother one morning very soon after was found dead, murdered in the most cold-blooded way. Poor mother! Dead. Murdered. The alarm was given by a servant early in the morning before I was awake. No one woke me. The housekeeper came to do so, but shrank away again pale and shivering: there was an impress on my arm of a bloody hand and fingers. My room was next my mother's; the door was open between us. What had happened I must have heard

had I chosen. Mamma had upbraided me
the night before about my sister's marriage; I had spoken to my maid in an
angry strain about it. The stain! So the
web closed round me.

'When the police came, the unusual
sounds had just aroused me. I felt heavy
and confused. Opening my door I called
my maid, who came trembling and in
tears. They told me what had happened,
but I did not realize it then. My manner
confirmed the terrible doubt everybody
present felt. It was a doubt with them
no longer. I was arrested and dragged
to prison. My room was searched of
course, and in the grate but half-con-
sumed was found my diary. On the last
written page, dated that awful night, was
a passionate threat against "the woman
who imprisoned me." The writing was
evidently mine, the clumsy destruction just
such as a girl would be doubly guilty of.

'But I need not lengthen the tale. The trial came. My advocate, powerful as he was, could not controvert such a mass of circumstantial evidence; he made the most of the inherent improbability of an affectionate young girl murdering her mother, but the judge disposed of that as evidence by telling of many cases when such things had been. So they doomed me to die. Rita had not been at the trial; her husband produced a certificate from two doctors saying that to give evidence would endanger her life. That grieved me more than anything. She was brave, I knew; for her not to come was to declare she thought me guilty. So I was careless about my fate; indeed, I prayed for death. As to the dishonour, to suffer was not more infamous than to be convicted.

'The day before the last she came. They had kept it all from her for fear of her health (as they said), but she had

found out just in time. There was something in her face I had never seen there
before, much more, I felt instinctively,
than sorrow, intense unspeakable as that
was, for my miserable fate. I noticed too
that she did not cry over me but for
herself, rocking backwards and forwards
on the hard wooden bench and moaning
piteously. Every now and then she
stopped crying to whisper, " You shall not
die, Eloise, you shall not die." She said it
so often that a wish for life seemed renew-
ed in me. I begged the jailor to retire one
moment, only while we said a last good-
bye. It was against the rules ; but there
were tears in his eyes, and he went—went
for perhaps three minutes. That was
enough to whisper to Rita what I wished
her to know, and to give colour to my
scheme.

'Next morning, when they came to tell

me the hour had come, I looked up and said, quietly,

'"Can you pardon my having deceived you, sir," (to the jailor) "thus, and to having taken advantage of your kindly absence yesterday to change places with my sister? Think, it was life I played for."

'The deception was perfect. No suspicion of my identity remained. Rita had, of course, not returned home the night before. They hunted for her everywhere, but in vain. She was hiding for my sake —alas! for more than my sake. Then in my new character I was tried again for felony in aiding a criminal to escape, but the court was compassionate and acquitted me.

'I should have told you that Rita's husband had been in court each day of the trial, had visited me during the awful time in prison at least once each day, and had in every way been strenuous to all appearance in his endeavours to alleviate my sad condition. In the providence of God, a fall from his horse detained him at home from the day of my interview with Rita until some little time after the conclusion of the second trial. Perhaps you understand why I say " in the providence of God ;" you will in a moment. My friends took me home. It was late. I dismissed them at the door, slipped down to the stable, saddled a horse myself (I was an excellent horsewoman), and before morning was across the frontier, eighty miles off. Thence I came to England, where I have been ever since.

'Now then, the worst is coming. You remember about the money. Our mother had made no will when she was murdered, so the money would have been equally divided between us ; but upon my conviction the half belonging to me was liable to confiscation by the crown. But, if I were dead before the estate was settled, all would go to Rita, or rather to Rita's husband. There was no fear of the crown enforcing its right under such circumstances. Well, from England I wrote, still keeping up my disguise, to my brother-in-law, and in a very few days he came over to me, thinking throughout it was actually his wife he was going to see.

'Having spent a few days with me, he went home, promising soon to return and bring Rita with him. He came alone, and in mourning deeper than that he wore for my mother. Rita was dead, he said. Why should I have disbelieved him? I knew no motive then he could have for deceiving me. He told me to call myself Rita still, or I should get no money, and that, though he would work for me always, still he was very poor. So, as though to Rita,

all the property was presently made over
to me.

'Some months later I married him.
From that instant he neglected me, loaded
me with insult and outrage. I think he
tried to make me die. We were rich, but
no income could withstand his extravagance. Two years brought poverty. He
did not mean to wait for that, but fate
overtook him. Before he died he told me
all—not repentantly, but for the pleasure
of the pain, the agony it gave me to be
told of it. Remember I loved him still,
passionately. He told me how *he* had
murdered my mother, while I lay, drugged,
in bed; how *he* had carried the corpse to
leave its finger-marks upon my arm; how
he had written the diary, carefully half
burning it. And then, worse, he told me
this: Rita, wondering that dreadful night
where he went, had followed him, not
there, but near enough to guess after-

wards the awful truth when he came home spattered with blood, and with a rosette from my mother's dress sticking to his sleeve like the brand of Cain—a relic of that terrible journey across the room with the speechless witness. That was what I had seen in her face in the prison cell. It was the determination to save me, even though to do so she should have to betray the fearful secret. Then afterwards she told him she knew, and refused to take the money, not even her own share, and threatened, if *he* did so, she would rather die—yes, let him die—than suffer me to be robbed. So he told her she must keep hidden yet some time, as I was still in France, and, professing the greatest abhorrence for his crime, came back to me in mourning, and did as I have told you. His last words were, " She may be alive yet for aught I know, and has probably not been living in luxury these last two years." Before he had time to die, God forgive me ! I struck him.'

No one spoke for a minute or two after Mrs. Grey concluded her narrative ; then Jonathan said, the new bent his mind was following asserting its supremacy,

' It is a mercy that, when he had you in his power on the occasion of your mother's murder, he did not murder you too.'

' The reason was obvious,' replied Mrs. Grey, quietly, ' the plan he followed promised to remove us both and at the same time to screen himself. To have killed me would have been clumsy as well as unnecessary ; so you understand—Jimmy—oh, don't be less kind to him for that.'

Jonathan rose, shook himself as if from a nightmare, and, walking across the hovel, kissed the pallid face of the little sleeper. He was trying to be himself again, and Heaven was helping him. How different might have been the years to come could he but have learnt from this poor woman's story all beneficence meant that it should teach him of motives misinterpreted and deeds misjudged.

CHAPTER VIII.

Some weeks later came a letter from Henry St. John, on the occasion of his return for the borough of Wotton-Basset. It ran as follows:—

'My dear Swift,

'I trust that time has, to some extent, at least, and in spite of my philosophy, rescued you from the severity of grief. At any rate you are much too good a friend and kindly a man—' Jonathan looked up from the sheet and ejaculated to himself, 'I believe he means it, and that our acquaintance justified him in that belief; I don't feel like it now,'—' to feel in the joys of others any aggravation of your own misfortunes : so I do not hesitate to expect a cordial congratulation when you know that three days ago the electors of the borough of Wotton-Basset returned me as their representative to Parliament. It will interest you, too, to learn that in order to this end I did not abate one jot or tittle of my independence of action. I am, as every member of a nominally deliberative assembly ought to be, a trustee absolutely unhampered by a single pledge.

'Matt Prior has gone to the Hague as attaché, or under-secretary, or something allied thereto, to the embassy. The post is worth £400 a year, so Matt has a fair chance of " doing well " (as they call it) in the world. Fancy the potentiality of extravagance being one's idea of well-doing ! Now, good-bye ; let me hear from you soon, and take care that the news be good. Every good fortune befall you— may I yet make bold to add—every happiness.

' Yours sincerely,

' H. ST. JOHN.'

That was all.

'A friendly note enough,' Jonathan thought, 'but good fortune will probably not befall me if my friends restrict themselves to wishing it may.'

He did not care much about the omission of all suggestion that his friend would not only be glad to hear of his success, but would strive to promote it; but he noticed it.   He, St. John, could get a secretary-ship of considerable value (for it was clearly his doing) for Prior; but he did not hint at doing anything for Swift. So Jonathan replied somewhat curtly as in view of any elegant, nicely-worded snub, and St.

John began to fancy **more than ever** that he
had too much allowed **his** friend's talents to
blind him to his faults of heart. **So** the
correspondence languished, indeed it was
months before another **letter** passed between them.   Nothing **could** have been
more unfortunate. **A** constant interchange
of ideas **with** such **a** man as Henry St.
John would **have** been **of the** greatest
possible value to Jonathan in the way of
forcing him beyond himself and obliging
him to follow other and brighter trains of
thought than those to which his circumstances inclined him.

As it was, there was nothing of the kind
to lighten his darkness. Hestor for **her
part** rightly judged that in giving direction **to his** energies, and a philanthropic
occupation to his spare time, she had sup-
plied the **best** medicine **in** her power to
offer. **So** she contented herself with
observing the gradual **progress her patient**

made towards recovery, and ceased to
inflict upon him what she imagined was
her unwelcome society. Jonathan saw a
good deal of her, nevertheless, more than
ever; but it was not on the same footing. They met now as co-workers in a
common cause, instead of as before, when
Hestor played the part of a vivacious
young lady demanding to be amused,
and Jonathan deferentially did as he
was bid. For Jonathan soon plunged
heart and soul into the task of reliev-
ing so far as was possible the misery
everywhere so plentifully to be met with if
one chooses to look. Of course, both to
him and to Hestor, Mrs. Grey and her boy
were the objects of greatest interest, but
they were far from being the only ones
whom their compassionate solicitude be-
friended. Almost every day Jonathan
found time to go to Woolham for an hour,
and very generally he managed to take

with him **some** such trifling delicacy for Jimmy **or his** mother as could be provided **out** of the pittance Sir William called his salary. **You** see he had nothing to do with it now-a-days beyond buying his clothes. **There was no one to work** for and send **it to,** and Jonathan Swift never **all his life** through loved **money for its own** sake. The time **was** coming when he **would** hoard, eagerly, greedily, but not for avarice.

'I can conceive,' he once said to Hestor, 'of a man whose soul **was** filled with **a** great pity **for** his fellows losing **all** hope for them, nevertheless ; but still, if he had the power, **he** would provide—for **the children and the lunatics.'**

Nothing, perhaps, conduces so much to **mutual** esteem between people **of** sense as transparent reality of conduct, chiefly, **I** suppose, because **people of** sense are wise enough **to** be transparently **real only at** the right time.   As a rule, it is a mercy that 'Art is man's Nature.' There are those, however, whose souls could be laid bare at any minute as baits to reverence and affection. Of such was Hestor Johnson, and of such I do not hesitate to say, in spite of the bitter darkness that was rolling in upon him, was Jonathan Swift. And, therefore, by the bedsides of the suffering, the dying ; amid the wailing of children who cried for food where there was none ; by empty grates where the shivering heaped curses upon the God of Harvests—places those, my readers, where there is generally very little artifice indeed—these two came by degrees, insensible degrees, to see as heaven had always meant they should. Unconsciously as yet, however ; but still an influence for good, and perhaps all the stronger and more beneficent for being unconscious. Heaven help the Positivists, those people who are

very estimable in the first generation.
They withhold credence from the incom-
prehensible! What is not? Certainly not
the French Republic! **Excuse** another di-
gression, **but I must.** How people who
allow themselves to use the word 'heat,'
for example, that being merely a force and
a thing no created being can explain except
by describing **its** effects, should grumble at
the word 'God,' would be marvellous except **for** the antiquity of the wonder (let
Comte be as modern as he will).

No thing is more certain than that **a**
belief in God has been all through history
a stronger force in the moral world than
heat has been in the physical; and
God for mortals must be their **belief in**
God.

The new rector of Woolham was an
elderly man of eight and twenty. It was
not his fault, poor fellow. He had been
elderly in knickerbockers. Some men are

so—not many. Therefore the fault is better than its opposite vice of being youthfully old. Heaps of people are *that*. I have a weakness for originality, and even original sin is better than nothing. A man is a man; and a clergyman is a man painted white and set up to be shot at. So I shall not abuse the rector of Woolham over much. To do so would seem like taking a mean advantage. The ordinary faults and follies of humanity should be gently dealt with in the case of men who are set, as it were, in the full view of detraction, and just for that very reason their extraordinary faults and follies should receive no quarter. When the Rev. Dr. Button, for instance, deliberately and of malice aforethought attends a political meeting, say on disestablishment, and in his speech displays ten times the venom and one hundred times the ignorance of most benighted and unchristian laymen on the platform, why **then** it **is time for** the public to cease attending the Rev. Dr. Button's church and listening to the **ex**hortations of one who is clearly a **knave** and a fool six **days out** of seven.

The rector of Woolham, **Mr.** Sawder, was not **at all** of this type; he was merely, as I have **hinted, a** man **at a** disadvantage, **and the** only difference probably between him and you, reader, **was** that, if he did not do less wrong than you, he was sorrier **for** it afterwards. Woolham was a good living, the parsonage an exceedingly comfortable **house, and** Mr. Sawder congratulated himself very much, when the **gift** of **it was** made **to** him, **on the sound** judgment **he** possessed, which had so successfully led him through **difficulties,** competition, and quicksands without number to **this** desirable **haven** of refuge. Being once there, he determined to remain there and to enjoy his good luck as fully as a calculating man can. So when fever broke out in his parish, just after his arrival, he was very much disgusted. Life was so distinctly preferable to an east window and a tablet, that he visited his sick parishioners as little as he decently could. Besides, he very soon began to doubt whether the poor, at least, among them cared much to see him. For that he was thankful: he certainly did not care to see them; and day by day the few visits wont to be made were more and more discontinued.

It was not till Hestor and Jonathan had for some weeks constituted themselves his curates and relieving-officers that Mr. Sawder ever even heard of them. At length, however, his casual orbit and their constant one so chanced to intersect that they met at the new quarters Sir William Temple had provided for Mrs. Grey. From that time the rector's interest in his parish seemed to develope wonderfully, as measured by the period spent on foot outside the rectory gardens. Hestor continually met him when on her errands of mercy, and not infrequently Jonathan, even when alone, did so too.

Now, Jonathan very soon discovered that he did not at all enjoy the Rev. Mr. Sawder's society. He did not mention the fact as a matter of principle. Clergymen to him, as their Master's servants, were not to be lightly spoken against; but the fact remained, nevertheless. Hestor, too, felt an instinctive dislike to the spiritual guardian of Woolham parish, and one day, as our hero and she were returning to Moor Park after visiting Jimmy, she expressed her sentiments on the subject with a directness which horrified her companion. Jonathan expostulated as well as mortal man could against the laughing sarcasms that took shelter behind such eyes, and tried very hard not to enjoy the reverend gentleman's castigation. He *was* enjoying it, nevertheless, perhaps all the more because of the consciousness that he was at any rate trying to do his duty, and the excitement of contest had made his eyes sparkle and the look of care seem comparatively slight on his brow, when who should come round the corner but the gentleman in question.

'Ah, Miss Johnson, how do you do? Mr. Swift, your servant. I am afraid I am late again. The irregularity of clocks and watches is really wonderful. It was my intention to have saved you the trouble of going your rounds to-day by going myself. But my new pony seemed out of sorts, and my watch must have stopped while I was doctoring him. Presently the people will think you are the rector, Mr. Swift, and I am merely ornamental.'

The tone of this last sentence, coupled

with the fact that it was said to a man
without the faintest pretensions to personal beauty, showed that the rector's
mechanically peaceable soul was stirred
from its normal condition. Indeed he
could scarcely help seeing that he was
somewhat in the way, and that is a very
irritating sensation to the best of men.
Jonathan merely smiled, but Hestor felt
indignant.

'Never fear, Mr. Sawder,' she said;
' your parishioners are not over bright.'

'Well, at any rate, I am too late for
to-day; so, if you will allow me, I will
walk back with you as far as the rectory,'
returned Mr. Sawder, who had no idea of
relinquishing his object. Of course Hestor
assented, and the walk was more agreeable
than might have been expected, thanks to
the good sense of Mr. Sawder, who was
determinedly complimentary to Jonathan
and submissive to Hestor directly the

policy of such conduct became apparent.

The rector of Woolham is only mentioned in this biography on account of the influence he exerted on the life of our hero, so I may be excused from recording the conversation in question. Of course he said nothing worth mentioning, and neither did Jonathan Swift. A clever man is only clever in clever society. A flint will not strike on wood, but, by the way, you can light wood on a flint. There are men, certainly, who rise superior to the chilling influence of a companion who is compounded of mediocrity, a good education, and a knowledge of figures; but they are those who can be *alone* in company. Blessed faculty to use society as a snail does its shell, and be enclosed by it without observing or being crushed by it.

The rector's reflections on his return home are, however, of consequence, at least so soon as the pony was revisited and re-doctored. For **Mr.** Sawder's thoughts **never** obtruded themselves **upon him;** he called them up, considered them, and dismissed them **again** by an infallible volition **at a** convenient season. But when there was nothing more~pressing **to do he** thought much as follows :

' This living is a good **one.** Even this **wretched season the income will be larger than I** require, though my tastes certainly **are** elegantly expensive. What shall **I** gain by saving? Nothing that I care about. It is not as though my tenure here were doubtful. No revolution can hurt *me,* **I am far too** moderate. **Well then, why should I not** marry? **A wife would** not be the nuisance to me she **is to many** men, simply because **from** the first **I** should go my own way and let her **go** hers. Besides, it would save me a lot **of** trouble—if I found the right woman—she could do all the **parish work, except funer-**

als and marriages, probably much better than I, too. So far, Hestor Johnson would answer perfectly. She is very pretty, *very* pretty. I think quite the prettiest woman I ever saw. That should not influence my decision in any way, but it is not to be despised, other things being equal. Now as to her position. When I was private chaplain to Sir James Carmichael, I was regarded as on a par with the upper servants—or at least there was not much difference in the distinction. Such is the way of the world in this enlightened seventeenth century. I have said grace in the buttery as well as in the hall, and that not such an aristocratic buttery as is Sir William's. Now, of course, I have got the upper hand of the upper servants, but then Hestor Johnson is on an exceptional footing. Her father was the trusted confidential steward for years, and, although she is a penniless orphan, Sir William's

countenance and protection more than
make up for that. She is going to live
soon at Manor Cottage as companion to
some old lady. I expect there will be very
little servitude about it. She certainly
likes that secretary fellow, that man Swift.
Mutual too, or I'm very distinctly mistaken.
After all, that doesn't matter, however, he
is very ugly and unusual. There is none
of that gentle uniformity and conformity,
so to speak, about him which women delight. A very short acquaintance with
me will make her forget him altogether.
He is startling, which is, being interpreted,
tiresome. One never can tell which way
the conversation will twist when he has
hold of its tail. Thank goodness, he
never has hold of its head while I'm there,
or I think it might bite. Let me see, it
is just possible Sir William may leave that
girl some money. He has certainly been
very kind to her. Well, so much the

better. There, that will do.' And the rector of Woolham proceeded systematically to think he would like a dish of tea.

CHAPTER IX.

AND so, as the weeks rolled **by, Jonathan's** better nature was being gradually drawn **back to** the world, to himself, **and, alas!** to suffering. For to restore to him joyous anticipation, hope, belief, was **not only to** again give him something to lose, but **it** was to open his eyes to the shadow walking beside him. **It** is difficult for those who **have never** experienced a **crushing** grief **to** realise the numbing effect **which** it has upon one's interest in all besides. **Sorrow is far** more absorptive even than joy, and most of us know how little room great happiness leaves in the heart for thoughts apart from its subject.

Through the thick night of his overpowering calamity, Jonathan's eyes had not marked the gaunt spectre born of the laurel-bush which was stalking beside him and waiting patiently for the daybreak. For long he was too crushed, careless, listless to waste a thought, much less a speculation, on the relations existing between Sir William and this pretty girl, young enough to be his grand-daughter. But love for her was flowing unconsciously in upon his soul, and the time was coming when he *must* think.

It was the late autumn. Sir William's great work on classical criticism was passing through the press, and Jonathan had his hands so full with correcting the proofs that there was not so much time for what Hestor (in laughing allusion to the career he proposed to himself) called his work on account, as there had been.

One day, having fairly worked himself

into a headache over some abominable details which mattered to no mortal man, he
strolled out to try the effect of some fresh
air, and before he was aware found himself opposite the scene of his faint and its
revelation.   He stopped uneasily.

'What am I to think?' he muttered.
'I had almost forgotten.   A plague upon
that raven!   What did it all mean?   She
is beautiful, so was Lauriel,' and the features stiffened painfully; but ere the question had time to rise, 'Is she no better?'
that question which would come so much
more darkly when the revelation had been
made to him that all the remaining love
of his great soul was given to this girl, all
the untorn fibres of his affection clinging
to her—ere, I say, he had time to frame
the question to himself, 'Is she no better
than the much-loved sister who resembled
her in so many ways?' Hestor's own bright
laugh had granted a reprieve.

'Now, Mr. Swift, if you have time to do nothing, you have time to escort me to Woolham.'

'On the contrary, that proves the impossibility,' he said, with an answering smile; the sun had got the better of the cloud for the time.

'Mr. Swift, those quibbles are beneath you.'

'Then they are very nearly all round me, for they certainly were before me, and will come after me; and, Miss Johnson, certain persons have sometimes heaped a good many upon me. I shall be most happy. It is a beautiful afternoon.'

'Dear me! are you also among those who talk about the weather?'

'It would not be civil of me to say,' he answered, 'you are the best judge.'

'Now, Mr. Swift, one more such wretched triviality and I shall retaliate.'

'No, no, that would be too tremendous. Please let me carry your basket.'

He stretched out his hand to take it, it slipped from his hold, and the bottle of wine for Jimmy which it contained was hopelessly broken.

'Oh! dear me, I am so sorry,' said Jonathan. 'What shall I do?'

'It is not of great consequence, Sir Clumsy,' she answered. 'Purcell will give me another to-morrow, and Jimmy has enough to go on with till then. No thanks to you, however. Well, now it isn't worth while to go. The next best thing is to climb the cone hill and to verify your brilliant observation on the weather from its commanding height. It is a pity, nevertheless, so I hope you are really sorry.'

The walk brought the memories of the past, so near and yet so distant, because divided by so dark a chasm from him now, crowding back upon Jonathan's mind. He had not ascended the cone hill since the

day when he first met Henry St. John :
that day when opportunity seemed at last
to place a weapon in the hand of genius.
He recalled the hopes he had founded
upon that encounter of an introduction to
the world which should enable him to
realise his noble ambition both for others
and himself, and, turning to Hestor, said,

'I hate suspense. It is the life of a
spider.'

'Translate it into " Hope," ' she answered, 'and it is the life of a God. Eternal
hope being eternally realised is the only
conceivable state of perfect happiness for
human nature.'

'Bravo,' he laughed, 'you have constituted a Britannic paradise with a vengeance, and made grumbling beatific !
What a motto for everlasting felicity !—

> " Grumbling for it
> When we've not it,
> Grumbling o'er it
> When we've got it." '

'Very well, then; what would you do? Lie before a fire and purr like a cat and be contented?'

'I should like to be contented, but I don't see much advantage in purring like a cat.'

'Sheer conceit,' she laughed, 'it is only because you want to purr originally. Yes, it is a beautiful afternoon.'

Jonathan's brow was smooth again. The bitter tone in which he had said, 'I hate suspense,' had died away. Hestor's half solemn, half sunny conversation had a wonderfully exorcising influence over his dark angel.

'Nature rejoices,' he said. 'By the way, what magnificent poetry that expression is, and yet, simply because it was first uttered some thousand years ago people have almost forgotten it is poetry at all. It is a pity they forget. For though, you know, in my opinion poetry is a special sense given to few, and that the balance of mankind can no more appreciate it than the blind can colour, still if they would remember a few such things they might serve as the blind man's dog serves. Nobody then would be deluded into believing that the author of such a preface to a poem as this—"I venture to place in your hands this book, the most mature of my works, and the one into which my highest convictions upon Life and Art have entered"—could be guilty of writing poetry except by mistake. A person who deliberately sits down to record his "deepest thoughts on men and life" (?) may write a very good philosophical work in rhyme; but the chances are against there being any poetry.'

'Where did you see that?' asked Hestor.

'In a vision of the nineteenth century,' he replied, 'when I expect the philosophy will be so bad that rhyme will be a God-send to it.'

'Talking of philosophy,' she said, 'Mr. Sawder expressed a mild surprise that I had not read somebody or other, I forget his name now. Mr. Sawder had met him in some great house in London. Everyone thinks very highly of him. To be perfectly frank, I had never heard his very name before. Was I grossly ignorant?'

'Be reassured,' said Jonathan, 'Mr. Sawder has, as I happen to know, never read "Spinoza." There are, no doubt, special reason in his case, but as a rule people who are well-read in living authors are literary snobs, they are people who read to talk of their reading and insinuate the height of their culture. While there is one book, sanctioned by the testimony of years and a long consensus of opinion, left to read, it is absurd to waste one's time by more than merely dipping into the unwinnowed harvest that has just been reaped. People are often ashamed not to be " well-read" as they call it, though goodness knows the adjective is very often scarcely suitable, in a heterogeneous mass of contemporary tom-foolery precisely analogous to that of the age before, which is universally forgotten. My own plan is to read as short a treatise as I can procure by anybody who is apparently springing into fame, and if I don't like it I trouble about him no more.'

'Come,' said Hestor, slyly, 'that is merely a piece of indirect civility, designed to sooth my injured self-love ; acknowledge it !'

'Not at all,' he replied. 'On the contrary, I fear I am never decently civil, and really, Miss Johnson, you have been kindness' self to me ever since I came here.'

Hestor blushed a little. She would

have laughed out some extravagance about being a good Samaritan, but that that line of reply might be too nearly true for pleasantry; so she looked mock-serious and said,

'I believe I have, Mr. Swift, and what has been my reward? Not so much as a copy of verses, and Hestor such an easy word to rhyme with, too. If the natural suavity of my temper didn't prevent me, I should make use of some very strong expressions.'

Jonathan held up his hands deprecatingly.

'I *did* write you some verses once,' he said, 'but they were half in fun.'

The tone in which he said it was such that Hestor thought it wiser to suppress the rising banter.

'I suppose now you would cut out the serious half and say simply "oh," instead.'

'Yes, but I shall write you some others as worthy of you as I can make them. I can do it better now than I could then, for many reasons.'

'It is very irritating to improve,' returned Hestor, with a malicious little laugh; 'it destroys one's self-confidence. The absoluteness of one's present perfection becomes doubtful under the circumstances, doesn't it?'

She thought she had successfully laughed-in a new subject, but Jonathan Swift was not so readily managed.

'Not yours,' simply, and with obvious sincerity, was the reply.

The tone brought the colour to her cheeks again, and forced her to take refuge in the phrase which has, I suppose, been more often used under the circumstances than any other.

'Don't talk nonsense.'

He was looking at her very earnestly,

and could **not help**, unobservant **in** the
small sense as he was, seeing her embarrassment. He had been speaking out **of**
the abundance of his heart, without **the**
least consideration of the why and where-
fore. Now, it flashed across him what he
was doing: he paused. Would that he
had **trusted the** God within him and **defied**
his reason, **his** senses, to inspire him with
a single doubt. **Would that he** had told
her how he loved her, and **she** had pledged
herself to him before **the** knowledge, coming, alas! so soon, had forbidden the
banns for ever! He sinned. He **was**
silent ; and his fate was fixed.

There was such **a** long pause that when
he said, ' **All** except " Hestor," ' it was an
effort to recall to what he referred. ' **I
do** n't **like the name,'** he went **on.**
' **Why, I** cannot tell, &c. It is not pretty
enough for you **by** any **manner of** means,
perhaps that is why.'

Quite as pointed as anything that pre-ceded, you may say. True, but the tone! That was different as day from night. Hestor's embarrassment all passed away, and a little pain nestled in her heart instead as she answered,

'Never mind that, re-christen me in the celebrated verses.'

'May I call you Stella?'

'Oh certainly, and thank you very much,' with a rippling laugh.

But there was something in the fiction which did not please her nevertheless. Poor Stella!

CHAPTER X.

JONATHAN had fully awakened to the fact that he loved Hestor Johnson, so there was no possibility of longer evading the question which stood between him and it. There were only two courses open to him. He could trust his better nature which told him Stella was as angelically pure as she was angelically beautiful, or he could set himself to work to 'think out' the scene by the laurel, and put two and two together and wonder and doubt—pugh! He chose the latter. It would not have been so before Lauriel was lost to him. His pure nature then might have wondered

but never doubted. What a wrench that
fancied fall had given to his every faculty!
Having so chosen, he was lost. The difficulty grew larger and blacker the more he
pondered it. Every instance of her in-
fluential beneficence to himself, those fairy
wand-touches, about which he had once
written laughingly home to his lost sister,
came back to him in dumb evidence of
evil.

He recalled the first hours of his stay
at Moor Park. It was she who had
told him, when his errand had obviously
failed, 'Sir William wishes to see you
again before you go.' Success had come
then. And then the evidence in chief,
the laurel scene : ' I shall be so sorry to go
away from you and from Moor Park.' The
steward's daughter to the steward's master!
' If the world should know I am no better
than other men.' The master to the servant's child! So the weeks rolled by, each

day burning-in the terrible suspicion deeper and blacker. At first it was only a **some-thing**, a cloud, a darkness. He would **not** let it take a definite shape. Against that he fought, struggling. It was bad enough **to** wonder, what does it mean? to reply would have been accursed. But under such circumstances **there is** generally somebody to help.

Given a knave and **some** knavery, or a saint and some knavery, anybody so long **as** he is about knavery, and **how** much assistance will he get? **I** do not know ; but there was a majority of forty-two the other day in favour of Local Option. If **I** live **and do not** find it too tiresome, I shall **some** day lead the party of ' Free **Will.' Our principle will be** that parliament is not **superior** to God Almighty, whose law it is that to add slavery to sin by enforcing righteousness is a wicked imbecility. To **compensate which, the** transgressors shall have a troublesome time of it under my administration.   Would I were Chief Secretary of Ireland just now.   County Cork should be Ulster over again within the fortnight.   It is wonderful what one can do with ten thousand troops who have been well stoned if one cuts the telegraph wires, refuses to obey instructions, and is prepared to face the consequences.   Oil of Rhodium is an infallible bait for rats.   The connection of ideas has led me away.   I remarked there is generally somebody to help a man situated as Jonathan at this time was.   And agreeably to the general principle so it chanced.

The Rev. Mr. Sawder, taking an unknown quantity of interest in Stella (I shall always call her so now) which he probably mentally put down as equal to x, began to notice curiously various little circumstances concerning her which would otherwise most likely have escaped him.   These had become **exceptionally** obvious **to** him while he was engaged in considering what chance there was of Sir William **leaving** his orphaned charge some money, **and how much.** It had then become **so evident that** he would, **and a** great deal too, that **Mr.** Sawder had judiciously subpœnaed **the** reason **why. The** negative result **of** his **inquiries had not a** little astonished him : X was evidently equal to z, z being Sir William's duty, affection, something **or** other, **and the size of** z puzzled Mr. Sawder sadly. **He** wondered **at first** whether Jonathan had anything **to do with it, just as** the world afterwards wondered, **but** he **was shrewd enough to see that that was not so,** without much consideration. **The more abstruse** the question became, **the more Mr. Sawder** quietly determined to find out **the** answer. **An** edge **of temper, too, was** gradually **being added to** his **investigation.**

There is a limit to the endurance of a quadratic equation, whether or not it goes on two legs, and Mr. Sawder was daily more and more annoyed to discover that his attentions were virtually thrown into the deep sea. He began to dislike Jonathan from the bottom of his heart, not very much, therefore, but somewhat. Such was his state of mind when one day late in November he chanced to spy Jonathan striding rapidly down the high road past the rectory.

'Mr. Swift,' called the rector, 'Mr. Swift, can you come in for a minute, if you please, I am anxious to have a talk with you.'

It was done as nearly as anything ever is done, on the spur of the moment, and so also was a good deal that followed. Devils and angels are equally scarce among men, and therefore deliberate malice is as rare as impromptu loving-kindness. It would have startled Mr. Sawder very much, just then, had you told him that within the next half hour he would be guilty of a great crime.

Jonathan deferentially assented.

'Have you read it? Good, isn't it?' said the rector, holding up a book so as to show the title, and not exactly knowing what to do by way of introduction.

'Yes,' returned Jonathan, 'but it would be better if it were not so clever.'

'Eh? Do you mean—let me see; how can that be?' queried Mr. Sawder.

'I daresay that isn't exactly what I mean,' answered Jonathan. 'I am a poor hand at expressing myself correctly.'

'Ah, you have a partiality for an unknown quantity. Well, so have I,' remarked Mr. Sawder, with a double meaning which was lost upon our hero.

'Certainly. Spoken language, even when used by its greatest master, is a nuisance altogether. It is impossible to make it sufficiently the vehicle of thought as opposed to the vehicle of itself, of language. I can't help thinking that a language of gesture would have been an—I was going to say " unspeakable," but that would savour of a joke—an enormous advantage to mankind. The less concrete the medium of thought the less ideas will be damaged in transmission, and the more chance there is that the recipient will receive what was despatched to him.'

' That would be hard on books,' said Mr. Sawder, anxiously on the look-out for a convenient opportunity to open fire.

' Books ! Oh, books don't matter, but conversation is worth living for.'

Here was a chance of which the reverend gentleman took immediate advantage.

' That depends so very much on one's companions and friends; for, after all, it

is not always the friends one loves best
whose society one most enjoys. Character
has a great deal to do with the awarding
of one's heart, but to a well-regulated
mind it has no influence whatever on the
enjoyment to be derived from a certain
society.'

'You are right, no doubt,' said Jonathan, 'but my mind is not well regulated.
All the suavity of manner, grace of person, comprehensiveness of mind, and scope
of imagination in the world embodied in
him could never reconcile me to spending
half an hour with Judas Iscariot.'

'Ah, that is a limiting case,' pursued
the rector; 'but there are many people
who are what we call "indifferent." Your
gesture language would be valuable here.
We know what bad means and what good
means, but, if "indifferent" comprehends
all betwixt the two, it might as well mean
nothing. Besides, very often we doubt

and wonder about a person without being able to say to which class even of these comprehensive ones he should be consigned.'

Jonathan looked uneasily at the speaker.

'Undoubtedly,' he said. 'Even men—and women—about whom the rest of their acquaintance entertain no doubt or question one way or other. Certainly—sometimes——'

'I am afraid few characters will bear too close an investigation,' continued Mr. Sawder.

'A mirage is always white,' answered Jonathan, with bitter acquiescence; and then, with an effort to be himself, he added, 'God knows. It is better not to think of it.'

Just then the thought occurred to Mr. Sawder—

'This man, in spite of my calculations, may be a dangerous rival. He is transparently honest, transparently high-minded. **He** may be trusted **not to** make **an** improper use **of anything I may say,** therefore I will be more than **frank; I** will tell him plainly what **I fear.** My doubt is a hazy **suspicion. I will intensify** it in the telling. It may deter his competition. I believe it will, and I may be wrong after all.'

So he answered,

'Yes, it is better **not to** think **of it** when in justice it can be avoided; but that is not always. Cases may occur when the consideration of our neighbour's character is necessary for our own peace and well-being. Such **a** case has actually occurred to me, and **it** is about it I wish to speak to you, as you are in **a** position to assist me as can **no one else.'**

Jonathan turned **very** cold.

'It was not at first my intention to do more than ask you a few questions, **in the** hope you would be good enough to answer them blindfold. I shall be perfectly frank, however. To be so, is due to you and to myself.'

He paused for an answer, but Jonathan only bowed.

Accepting what encouragement he could get, Mr. Sawder went on :

'The few months of my residence here have afforded me ample opportunity to justly determine whether Miss Hestor Johnson is a suitable person to become my wife except in one particular. She is amiable, sympathetic, charitable—indeed, to a superficial on-looker, she is perfection itself.' Another scarcely perceptible bow. 'But there are some scarcely explicable circumstances in her life (that is, on any hypothesis I care to consider). I heard incidentally that Sir William has not always been as obviously kind to her as of late years. There was a perceptible change in the relations between them after the death of her mother.'

Jonathan started. This was news to him, and terrible news too.

'It is surely reasonable that his kindness should increase with the need for it,' he answered, manfully.

'To a certain extent,' replied the rector. 'Yes, within limits ; but, you know, there are limits. Her influence with him is very great. Mrs. Grey's new cottage *must* have been her doing or yours. Sir William never did such a thing in his life before, and I think you told me it was not yours ?' A bow again. 'I thought so. Well, what is the alternative ? An explanation there must be. The greater the difficulty of getting it, the greater the hazard as to what it will be when it come. Can you give it to me ? You know my position and my right to ask. You can scarcely have lived at Moor Park so long and not seen cause for suspicion, if suspicion is justified.'

Then Jonathan Swift rose superior to himself in his love and anger.

'She is as pure as an angel,' he said, 'as white as snow. You are infinitely unworthy of her, and, God knows, so am I.'

CHAPTER XI.

A FEW days after the interview recorded
in the last chapter, Mrs. Dingley arrived
at Manor Cottage, and Stella at once entered on her new duties as that lady's
companion. Little had been said about
the approaching change before it came,
for Jonathan always felt himself guilty of
implied equivocation when forced to listen
to Stella's story without replying, ' Thank
you, I know all that, and more than that;
I heard it by accident months ago, when
Sir William told you.' So he had seemed
almost to rudeness careless of this new
arrangement, and although Stella repre-

sented it (as she was bound under the circumstances to do) as a rise in life and a thing to be delighted at, yet Jonathan would never condescend to sully the whiteness of his truth by the endorsement of a congratulation. As for himself, he could not make up his mind whether he was glad or sorry she was going. Passionately anxious to read her heart, he would have her constantly beside him. Half convinced he had deciphered it already, he wished her very memory away.

Poor little Stella could see enough of this to make her very unhappy, though the reason, of course, she never guessed at. She knew, as a woman always knows, that Jonathan loved her, loved her deeply, loved her with all the remaining love the broken casket of his heart contained ; but she could see, too, that that was not all.

'There is something between us,' she used often to sadly think, as she saw the cloudy care that **not even** *her* sun could pierce come drifting over his face. 'What interposing rock is it which makes me cast a shadow on him instead of brightness?'

More than ever she had been thinking thus during the first week of her **new life** at the **Manor** Cottage. Jonathan **had not** been **guilty of even the** civility of **a call.** What did **it mean?** Presently a brilliant idea occurred to **her.** He was poor, miserably poor, to all intents **and** purposes a pauper. That must be the reason. Her lip curled a little when the notion struck her.

'Ah, he supposes **I** am for sale. Natural enough, certainly—girls pretty **generally** are. **It is not his** fault that **human** nature is very contemptible, or that **he** reasons from human nature.'

This would **be a capital** opportunity to **rail at the** worshipping of **Mammon, and** especially, **being a loyal subject of the old** type, who would die in the last, or any other ditch, to do him a service, at a very great personage for hob-nobbing with a lot of German Jews, who are distinguished from old-clothes-men merely and solely by their great possessions. *Therefore* I neglect the opportunity. And besides, not Thersites himself could object to wasting an opening of such constant recurrence. To proceed, however. Stella thought over what she should do, and decided, in accordance with common sense, that she would, so far as maidenly self-respect permitted, put it in Jonathan's power to undeceive himself.

One of the few good points in modern conventionality is its stern condemnation of the woman who woos, and your ‘ reasonable ’ people are apt to force that to its apparently logical conclusion and mete out proportional retribution to the woman who nearly woos. Common-sense, however, is

knowing when the illogical is right, and
Stella trusted **its** inspiration. Of course
the real basis of the whole matter is the
chivalrous and perfectly correct **opinion**
that a gentleman should never say ' no ' to
a lady ; and therefore **a** woman **may** woo
just so **far as** tacit **refusal** shall not imply .
an insult. Stella, without troubling her
head about the ' real basis ' any more than
about the origin of matter, **did** what was
right. She sat down and wrote Jonathan
a frank little note ostensibly about Mrs.
Dingley, and how astonished that worthy
gentlewoman was that Mr. Swift had never
dropped in to drink a dish of tea. Then
she **went on to say** he must **call on** pain of
her displeasure, and ended up with a
pretty lecture about considering himself
more than others.

The day after receiving this epistle,
Jonathan trudged with a very unwilling
heart to Manor Cottage. He went be-

cause no available excuse for not going offered itself, and therefore it would have been rude to stay away; but it will enable you, reader, to understand some of the turmoil in his breast when I say that this penniless, friendless man, the product of continual failure, was anxiously considering as he walked along the dusty highway whether he would not quit the shelter of the only roof he could count upon to cover him, simply to escape the presence of this woman whom, nevertheless, he passionately loved. Try to realise the circumstances, try to conceive of the man—and then fill your souls with the tenth part of an iota of what he felt.

A sound of scampering hoofs behind the hedge roused him from his bitter ponderings, and in another instant Mr. Sawder's pony, which had been turned out to grass for the benefit of his health, cleared in sheer wantonness the hedge which divided his paddock from the road. He was a small, but very handsome sorrel grey. Jonathan looked at him admiringly for a moment, and then remarked,

'Well jumped, Mr. Horse; you have the advantage over me. *I* could not have cleared that hedge. However, let me console myself; you are not so distinctly superior to my brother the monkey!'

Alas! for it, the tide of bitter doubt was rising fast again, and it was bitterer than ever. Then, the pony suffering himself very unconcernedly to be caught, Jonathan led him round to the yard. Mr. Sawder was there. Jonathan sneered in spite of himself. Mr. Sawder was *always* in his stables.

'Here is one of your parishioners, Mr. Sawder,' he said. 'I caught him in the act of turning dissenter, and, as you see, have brought him back to church. You had better give him a sermon or some oats —either will do.'

'Thank you, Mr. Swift, I am infinitely obliged, I am sure. Jumped out of the paddock, did he? Here, William, hobble Conrad before you let him out again. Come in and drink a glass of Burgundy, Mr. Swift. No! well, never mind, better luck next time. Pardon my asking, but if you are going to Manor Cottage, there is a much shorter cut through my kitchen-garden.'

Jonathan bowing assent, the vicar strained his courtesy to the length of leaving Conrad in charge of the groom, and himself showing the way.

'There, you see,' he said, when the gate was reached, 'there, straight across the fields, there are stiles everywhere. It is not more than half a mile from this; and, pardon me one moment, Mr. Swift, have you been there before?'

Jonathan shook his head.

'Very well, think honestly after this visit whether there is not more foundation for the warning I gave you than you were disposed, when I saw you last, to admit. Tell me, when you have seen the house and understood Miss Johnson's position in it, whether any sane man ever did as much for the *ugly* daughter of an old servant. Besides' (with a look of conscious merit), 'she is certainly a terrible flirt.'

This last clause was a deliberate falsehood, and to do the reverend gentleman justice he was very much ashamed of himself two minutes later for having been so vulgarly wicked. The spasmodic repentance was no antidote, however, for the poison of the lie. That did the work it was sent into the world to do, famously. It is odd to remember that the results of that lie are not dead yet. Remember that until this moment there had been no touch of jealousy in Jonathan's soul. He had doubts, fears, miseries enough in all conscience, but not that one; this spirit

was far too noble to love what was bad
or consequently to be jealous about what
was bad. He was not one of those
psychological curiosities who can swear to
love, cherish, and esteem a criminal from
the divorce court. It was a new pang to
him to learn, on the authority of one whose
very profession was truth, that even if the
shadow which oppressed him should prove
but a shadow still his divinity was—a flirt.
This made him angry ; the other had made
him sad.

Jonathan was heartily glad of it when
he reached Manor Cottage and the exi-
gencies of conversation obliged him, if not
to forget the main idea which occupied his
mind, at least to think of other things as
well. Mrs. Dingley took his fancy very
much ; she seemed sensible, agreeable,
and accomplished, and altogether such a
person as he would have wished for Stella's
guardian.

' I wonder how far she is in the secret,' he thought, ' and what is the relative position of the two ladies when strangers are away ?'

' This is a pretty room, Mr. Swift,' prattled the lady about whom he was thinking. ' Sir William was most kind to do it up so nicely for me, remembering that I pay a most trifling rent. The house would let now, I feel convinced, for twice the money. You see,' she went on, ' I am a connection of his, and perhaps he thinks that even a very little blood is thicker than water. My dear ' (addressing Stella), ' you know best, but it seems that Mr. Swift and you have been very good friends, so perhaps it would not bore him to peep into the dining-room and garden, just to see what kind of a nest you have come to, would it ?'

' Thank you very much,' said Jonathan, ' it will give me great pleasure.'

'Well then,' continued Mrs. Dingley, 'if you will excuse my assistance, Hestor, I will spend five minutes in writing a note, and beg Mr. Swift to send it when he goes back by Sir William's post-bag. Mind, Mr. Swift, the verdict is to be "perfection."'

So the two went together to admire the new home.

'It certainly is very pretty,' said Jonathan, with a weary sigh that poor Stella altogether misinterpreted as she answered with a laugh,

'Would you have liked it less so? You see, it is not as though these things were mine. I am as poor as I can be. There is no fear of luxury making me its victim. I should despise myself if I could not be quite as happy without these trappings as with them.'

'And yet thousands of women would go through fire and water for these "trappings," as you contemptuously call them,' remarked Jonathan.

'And thousands would do nothing of the sort.'

'Ah, of course; there are a great many who do not need to do so.'

'Mr. Swift, if I did not know you better than you know yourself, I should despise you.'

Jonathan turued and looked curiously at the flushed face and sparkling eyes. Could this possibly be mere acting, nothing more than au episode in an organized deception? Certainly not. To suppose so was wilful blinduess; but he was not convinced. He would not surrender the evidence of his senses at the bidding of a sparkle and a gesture. That is to say, he insisted on preferring, in spite of himself, second-hand impressions before intuitive fact. These 'trappings,' the flowers, the vases, the elegant furniture,

Mrs. Dingley herself, were all before him there under the same roof, forbidding him to believe that the scene beside the laurel was a dream, forbidding him even to hope so.

'Then this at any rate follows beyond all question,' Jonathan thought to himself, as he watched the lustrous eyes grow quiet again and the flush recede beyond its wont towards pallor—'this at any rate follows: she is certainly living here under a false character. She is the lady of the house; she pretends to be a sort of servant. She is—never mind. I will force myself to forget her. She is no better than poor Lauriel was, my poor little sister.'

Stella wondered at his silence. Her heart beat fast. Was he making up his mind to say what a woman so loves to hear—that she is loved? How little she guessed what it was he pondered!

'That is a pretty picture,' she said at last, pointing to one before them, 'but I don't know what it represents. Can you tell me?'

The picture was this: A tawny, beautiful youth, bearing in his arms a lovely maiden, whose love-lit eyes were turned away from him, was striding rapidly along with his burden. Crowds of men and women, youths and maidens, opposed his progress and snatched at his burden, but the painter had admirably portrayed the impotence of their endeavours, and the spectator could see that the tawny lover possessed a power all his own. A murky river that gleamed strangely was seen in the distance, one could scarcely see whether near or far, and the wine spilt from a goblet the beautiful maiden was carrying ran down and mingled with it.

'That is "Death and Pleasure,"' said Jonathan.

'How can that be? Pleasure surely is not in the arms of Death. He comes behind her.'

'Think again,' replied Jonathan. 'Is not this ideal much higher than that? Is it not true that all human pleasure—all pleasure, I mean, but the divine one of glorifying God, depends for its very existence upon Death. You see, he has taken her from *these*, but he is bringing her to *those*. Is it not true he does so? Is it conceivable that man, at once immortal and sinful, could know such a word as pleasure? Do you really believe that the amusements, paltry and worse, of this petty term would continue to please through myriads of centuries? Do not they pall and weary in three score years and ten? Oh, how utterly! No, no, it is Death which prevents men from becoming mere inanimate lumps, and secures that they shall, at any rate after their own fashion, and for a little while, live their lives and enjoy them. I promised Stella some verses once and left the promise unfulfilled,' he went on. 'If she will allow me, I will write a couple of stanzas to her picture instead; the painter deserves it, for he is a poet, which is as unusual for a painter as for most men.'

Picking up a pencil, he wrote hurriedly as follows:

' Fair, oh, fair as the soul's creation
   Of some great poet; oh fair! how fair!
   Pour to her honour a deep libation,
   While laughter ripples among her hair;
   And the wishful, tremulous, glancing flashes,
   Like death-lights dancing beneath her lashes,
   Sending the waves of their living quiver,
   Gleam for gleam, to the gliding river,
   While the trickling wine drops' mingling stream,
   Answers in ecstasy gleam for gleam.
   And the mighty youth, in whose arms reposing,
   Half unknowing through great delight,
   She lies, each gesture, each glance disclosing
   Something beautiful, something bright.
   Drink, too, to him, so sublime in his seeming,
   Bearing his burden as though he were dreaming,

Striding so easily down to the river,
Though strength resist, and though beauty shiver ;
Murmuring languidly, Pleasure saith,
Drink to me.   Ay!   But to her—and Death.'

'Thank you,' said Stella.   'It is very pretty, but it is very horrible.   I wish, Mr. Swift, you *could* not have written that.   It would be better to be more stupid, if so you would be more happy;' and the great eyes were turned regretfully to his.

'Poor child,' thought Jonathan, as he looked pitifully back.   'I am happier than she, after all.'

Then very soon they parted, and he went his way blinder than ever, bitterer than ever; and with the last quivering remnant of his belief in human nature almost crushed out.

CHAPTER XII.

THE reader may be surprised that, under the circumstances, Swift condescended **to** set foot again in Moor Park, and indeed **it was** very indicative of what his experience was bringing him to, that he did not shake the hated dust from his feet, and seek elsewhere those virtues **to** which **his** master's mansion was apparently a stranger. Had **he** considered Sir William **to be a** bad man, he would have gone away; the misery was that he had **learnt** to consider him to be an ordinary man. And why should he hunt for the day in Tartarus? The vials **of** his **scorn could be** poured out equally well at Moor Park as elsewhere, and the only positive wish left in his heart was to pour out those vials.

Such was the spirit in which he sat down directly he got back from Manor Cottage to write 'Gulliver's Travels,' and one Yahoo's hovel was as good as another for the purpose. The Yahoos were hateful, and if he could not make them better, he would, at any rate, paint their hideousness for his own sad gratification. It was a necessary consequence of this state of mind in the case of so upright and manly a nature as was Jonathan Swift's, that showing even ordinary respect and deference to his fellows, and especially to those whom the world was pleased to call his betters, became a matter of great difficulty. He detested pretending to look up to those on whom, in point of fact, he looked down, mentally and morally, and the result was obvious in his conduct.

I hope I have made my own position quite clear as to this, but perhaps I had better assure it further, as a biography and a eulogy is commonly supposed to be the same thing. Jonathan Swift was as far wrong as to the despicableness of human moral nature as he was right in despising the intelligence of nine hundred and ninety-nine men in a thousand. All I have been anxious to point out is that circumstances were such as to make his error easily explicable, and should lighten the severity of censure. You, too, will find it difficult, reader, to resist the souring influence of crimes which are against God—and you.

Sir William Temple at once noticed the change which had come over his secretary, and resented it in accordance with the promptings of a lofty and elegant sense of the young man's ingratitude. It is difficult to manage a man who has neither fears

nor hopes, however, and Sir William had
to choose between sending his secretary
away and putting up with the very scan-
tiest of ordinary civility. Jonathan had
gradually become a very indispensable
part of the establishment. He was the
only secretary the baronet had ever had
whose work suited him thoroughly, and if
the man was not quite after his own heart,
that, he thought, was of comparatively
little consequence. Besides, no one could
live long on terms of any intimacy with
Jonathan without being impressed with his
sterling character and single-mindedness,
and Sir William was wise enough to balance that against a good deal of eccen-
tricity of manner. Nevertheless, the relations between him and Jonathan were
occasionally strained, and they happened
to have been peculiarly so for some little
time, when one day, to the infinite surprise
of the latter, Matthew Prior drove up to

the big ornamental ironwork gates in his official capacity as secretary to the embassy at the Hague.

It was early spring. Jonathan happened to be standing at the gates, thinking, very sadly and bitterly, of all that had pased since they first were thrown open to him, when the carriage drawn by four first-rate post-horses, and otherwise in every way indicative of somebody being inside who was profoundly indifferent to travelling expenses, drew up before them. Prior saw him and at once jumped out to shake hands. True, his good fellowship with the gaunt ugly figure in dingy black had been very short and very sadly ended, but Prior was not the man to stick at a trifle like that. He had often heard of Jonathan from St. John, and knew the latter too well to dream of his being mistaken in his high estimate of Swift's ability. Besides, the secretary looked poor and wretched, while Prior was getting-on in the world and being of use to himself and other people. So, as I said, he jumped out and shook hands with him, asking cheerily whether the illustrious author of the **T. A.** was anywhere to be found? how the Bentley controversy was getting on? and how he, Jonathan, had managed to endure the cold winter in such a bleak place? with a hundred more questions diplomatically heaped on those so as clearly to indicate that the sad past was to be buried out of sight if possible. Jonathan shook hands warmly on the spur of the moment, and immediately afterwards felt rather ashamed of himself for having responded so easily to Prior's overtures.

'So much civility cannot possibly have been lavished on me for my own sake,' he thought. 'He wants something from Sir William, and fancies I can be of use. I have wasted a suspicion of human kind-

ness. Never mind, the imitation is not
generally so exact.'

Then translating his thought into conventional expression, he begged Prior not
to trouble to walk to the house. It was
some little way ; he had much better drive,
and so forth. But Prior was immovable.

'Bother the carriage. Bother the distance. Bother the big potter and his broken
plate. I've been sent to get his advice,
by the way : fancy anybody being in a
hurry for that—they can wait or go on, all
but the distance aforesaid, just as they
please. No, no ; if diplomacy is going to
prevent me talking to my friends, she
shall quit my service. Come, it's a beautiful day and as dry as your controversy ;
let us sit here behind this precious paral-
leliped that I suppose is the Moor Park
for tree. Thank God, there were no Dutch
assessors at the Creation. Ugh ! It
makes me shudder to think they were

even as near as the "Triple Alliance."'

'I beg your pardon, Mr. Prior,' interrupted Jonathan, 'but pardon my saying
it is unworthy of a true wit to joke about
his Creator.'

'Certainly; you are quite right. The
fact is, one says that sort of thing without
thinking. Upon my word, I believe I am
responsible for nothing that I say, and for
very little that I do, when I am in good
company and get my spirits up.'

Jonathan smiled a little at the idea of
his being ' good company.'

' Hi !' called Prior to a post-boy, ' take
that parable away, but first give me the
claret out of that basket in front there
and two glasses. We will have a good
chat before I fling myself into politics.'

' Here's the claret, sir,' said the post-
boy, coming back, ' but I can't find any
parable.'

' Take the carriage instead, then, to the

stables. Mr. Swift, why is a carriage like a parable?'

'Some vile pun, I suppose,' laughed Jonathan; 'something about that, when it is kept going "weal" goes all round, and when it stops all is "woe;" or something about its often being overdrawn and far-fetched; or else that it is frequently for hire objects—I don't know.'

'Pretty fair, pretty fair; my reason was much better—quite deserved the priority, but I've forgotten it. Well, then, tell me what are you doing. St. John speaks of you so often that I can't help feeling you ought to take as much interest in me as he does, while I certainly do *vice versâ*.'

'I suppose it is because St. John talks so much about me that he never has time to write,' remarked Swift, with a suspicious bias towards a sneer.

'Nay, you must excuse that, because the poor fellow is really very busy; he is fighting his way up in spite of the mediocrities who fancy that age and intelligence are convertible terms, but those people take a terrible lot of hammering.'

'I am glad to hear it,' returned Jonathan, 'for I hate those people beyond expression. But, after all, what can you expect? Chronology recommends itself especially to those who are incapable of anything else. Twice two is much easier than any other estimate—in fact, that is the only thing, poor wretches, they can be quite sure about. I know nothing about horses, so when I take a coach—seldom, certainly—I take the one with the biggest horse. Your elderly mediocrities know nothing about real brains, so on the same principle they choose the man with the oldest.'

'Bravo! bravo!' laughed Prior. 'Gall and wormwood for them, and richly they deserve it. I'll retail that to a certain Mr.

George Russell, a member of Parliament, and an acquaintance of mine, to whom it especially applies, and who the other day solemnly warned a cabinet minister not to reply to a speech of St. John's, because "an eagle is not prone to catch flies." By the solemnity of Moses, here's Sir William, or another elderly diplomatist, which is the same thing !'

'Yes, it is Sir William ; I will introduce you and be off.' Then, as the old gentleman approached, 'This is Mr. Prior, Sir William, whom probably you expect. He has been so obliging as to shake hands with me before going up to the house, as we met before some time back. I will leave him now, if you will allow me, in your charge.'

'What a fine fellow Mr. Swift is !' remarked Prior to Sir William, when Jonathan had left them. 'I don't know him very well myself, but Henry St. John saw

a good deal of him when he was here, and
he swears by him.'

'H'm!' said Sir William. 'He has
ability, certainly, but then it is not a
methodical ability. He is for ever sur-
prising one. Put him in never so straight
a road and he is sure to wriggle into a bye-
path from sheer preference, even if he has
to make the bye-path to wriggle into. A
man's mind ought to be like a horse in a
cart. Put it into the shafts, point it in a
certain direction, act upon it by certain
forces, and you know precisely where it
will go.'

A flippant allusion to the more exact
resemblance of such minds to asses,
whether in carts or out of them, was re-
pressed by poor Matthew with some difficulty, and he bowed deferentially.

'Besides,' went on Sir William, 'his
manner is so peculiar. There is a somewhat in the way in which he says the most

ordinary things which is repellant, defiant;
I had almost said—but it would be absurd
in this connection—contemptuous.'

'Indeed! Extraordinary!' ejaculated
Prior, wondering partly whether his highly respectable informant *really* thought it
would have been absurd 'in this connection,' and partly that Jonathan had no
deeper respect—not for the man, but for
his bread and butter. 'Most extraordinary!'

'So it is,' continued the worthy baronet,
'and it is a great pity. To judge by the
sarcastic bitterness of his speech one
would fancy him a misanthropist of the
deepest dye. Yet he is a kind-hearted
fellow at bottom. I saw him the other
day meet a beggar on the road. He looked furtively around him to be sure he was
alone—when I say the other day it was
some months ago. The weather was
bitterly cold. The beggar seemed dying

of cold. Mr. Swift emptied his pockets into the poor wretch's hand. There was but fourpence; but I think it was all he had in the world, and then, to crown all, he took off his coat, saw the beggar warm in it, and then cut across a back way home—though it took him up to his knees in snow—so that no one should find him in his shirt-sleeves and discover he was better than his professions.'

'I suppose that is what one understands by apostolic conduct, isn't it?' inquired Prior.

'Precisely,' answered Sir William; 'but you should have heard him that same evening demonstrating in the civilest manner possible—that is to say, in such a way that nobody had a fair claim to call himself insulted—that virtue was but a name, integrity an imposition, honour malice on a small scale, and patriotism simply enlarged honour. Well, since Mr. Swift has the honour of your acquaintance, I **will ask him** to dine with us to-night. There **will** be **a** considerable company **to meet you** ; for, desolate as this place **is, we** are **not** absolutely alone.'

Then politics supervened, **so we** will leave **them. I** object **to** politics. They are simply **a** question of good police. And international politics, which concerned our friends just then, I object to most of all. *They* are simply a question of a bad police. International politics mean national inefficiency.

CHAPTER XIII.

I APPEAL to my readers to acquit me of having wilfully wasted their time and my own by lengthy descriptions of the vernal equinox, or the moon's bright shimmer, or the lightning's lambent glow, or anything of that sort. And if I seem to be devoting a good deal of attention to the depiction of Jonathan's state of mind at this time I must plead that I only do so because the biography would be otherwise unintelligible. That is why I beg you, gentle readers, not to imagine for one moment that you can safely skip the chapter here following, which describes briefly the big dinner that Sir William gave in honour of the young attaché whose romantic advancement had been in everybody's mouth. Well, then, to proceed.

Jonathan was there covered, metaphorically speaking, with roses. He laughed and chatted in a way which amazed Prior. The conversation was of course, to begin with, about the weather and the bad winter, and thence by an easy transition it glided off to the coldest possible potentate, the Czar of all the Russias, and thence again by easy stages to Russian political cruelty and wickedness. An old peer present was very solemn in his demonstrations, and at last told a harrowing tale of some poor wretch who had been exiled to Siberia for life for not saluting the emperor's carriage, though it was empty.

'Ah,' remarked Jonathan, with a serious face, 'was not that the Duke Constantine Scobeloffschin?'

The antique peer thought that was so.

'Ah then,' said Jonathan, 'you have omitted the worst part of the case, probably out of respect for our feelings; the sentence was increased, on account of the defiant bearing of the criminal, to banishment during November to London.'

Everybody laughed but my lord, and he looked daggers, bided his time and presently turned the conversation, with the worst of taste, to the gradual obliteration of class distinctions and the evils therefrom resulting. He talked straight at Jonathan, and Prior was amused to watch the result. At the same time he could not make Swift out. He had been depressed, morose, savage that same afternoon, and now he was apparently diametrically the reverse. Prior watched his glass; he was drinking nothing. It was not that. It was an experiment. He was trying whether excitement would enable him to forget;

whether misery would not succumb to persistent laughter, and whether with jokes as pebbles he could not slay the Goliaths of Recollection and Hopelessness. I do not pretend he quite realized this himself. I think that people in his circumstances **very** rarely do quite realize the motives that inspire them. **That is the** psychological fact, however, and whether the utterance of the crushed spirit sounds like laughter or sighing is only an alteration, after all, in the disposition of the mortal combat **of** Nature against despair. Presently **Jona**than's turn came.

'I have known,' urged the peer, 'young men of no family, no means, no education presume to differ flatly even from me. **Yes, sir,** even young men whose ignorance and want of birth was such that they could not, dare not translate "**N**oblesse oblige."'

'Honour amongst thieves, isn't **it ?'** in**terposed Jonathan.**

The noble lord gasped, Prior laughed merrily. Sir William struck in, in defence of his guest, with a dignified, not to say contemptuous,

‘Certainly not, sir.’

‘Oh, dear me,’ answered Jonathan, ‘it is very hard upon Lord Soimême to tell him that his favourite French proverb means *Dis*honour among thieves. ’Tis really too bad.’

Then, changing the subject, he wheeled round upon his ‘patron’ and remarked, with an air which fully expressed an instant and absolute forgetfulness of his noble antagonist opposite,

‘Talking of thieves, there was mention made in the last London letter of some visionaries who have recently promoted meetings of what they call “reclaimed thieves.” They decorate these poor wretches with ribbands, get a couple of thousand people to look at them, make speeches to them, at them, and of them, play some music on a brass band, and then—send them home! What is your opinion, Sir William, of the virtue which depends for its existence on two thousand spectators, blue ribbands, a brass band, and a solo vocalist?'

'You are very much too deep for me, Mr. Swift,' was the chilling reply, 'I really cannot grasp the question.'

'My lord,' said Jonathan, instantly turning to the grandee opposite, 'are turnips a satisfactory food for cows?'

Sir William saw the connection of ideas and was angrier than ever. The noble lord did not. Presently Prior, during a general shuffle for the inspection of a work of art, found means to whisper, laughingly,

'*Noblesse oblige* our worthy host to be exceedingly savage.'

Jonathan turned on him almost fiercely.

'You laugh,' he said; 'you may, you can, but I'—and the bitter sneer in his voice fairly made Prior start—'*I* depend upon him for my bread and butter! *I* am the recipient of his bounty. He inspires my stomach. I shall be starved. Down, Tozer, down; crouch, Tozer, crouch. Good dog!!! Stay, I *will* laugh, I *must* laugh: pass me the claret.'

Then Prior's attention was called off to a squeaky old gentleman, who had exhausted his vocabulary of admiration on Sir William Temple's new picture of a Dutch Jupiter casting amorous glances at a Dutch Venus, and wished to start a brand new hare to hunt with the same dogs. It is wonderful how many people in the world do this. They have the same idea for all subjects, just as there are accompaniments guaranteed to fit all songs and perorations to fit all speeches. Of course the universality of their application makes them lose a little in distinctiveness, but what does that matter to ordinary conversation?

'Holland is a very beautiful country,' said the squeaky old gentleman, 'very beautiful indeed, is it not, Mr. Prior?'

Prior assented with a diplomatic insinuation about the want of an occasional hill.

'True—ah, true, that must be very ugly, very ugly indeed,' looking puzzled.

Matthew civilly suggested the windmills as a reason for his interrogator's original opinion.

'Ah, yes, the windmills, of course, the windmills;' and then, seeing an opening for his one idea, 'you see, they must necessarily be more beautiful than mountains or rivers, or—or—or—that sort of thing, because they suggest men while the others suggest nothing but inanimate nature.'

The same thought had been tagged on

to the picture, the eatables, everything.

'You are eminently right, sir,' put in Jonathan; 'there is nothing better calculated to suggest most men than windmills.'

'You are a cynic, sir, a cynic,' said the squeaky old gentleman.

'Remember, sir, a cynic is a man who prefers inanimate nature.'

'Worse than that,' shouted the hero of *noblesse oblige*; 'a cynic is a man who judges of others by himself.'

'I suppose,' remarked Jonathan, 'that that accounts for the fact that cynics are always low-born people. No true aristocrat would ever think of judging others by *himself*. It would be so absurdly complimentary.'

Said with every necessary appearance of conviction, the opinion could not be distinctly objected to, and the earl retired to his entrenchments, firmly resolved to let

Sir William, at a more convenient season, know what he thought of asking contemptible whipper-snappers to dinner.

Sir William himself was waxing angrier and angrier. Prior mentally calculated the chances of an open rupture (after his new kind, as a diplomatist), and what would become of Jonathan in that event (after his old kind, as the embodiment of good nature and considerate feeling). The squeaky little gentleman was laboriously contriving a new application of his idea: port occupied some minds; claret occupied others. These are the premonitory symptoms of politics. Politics are a sort of German hospital for conversational destitution. Presently somebody hinted 'that was a great debate,' and then they all talked long and furiously about how great or little it was. There was a statistician present: I suppose there always will be until the millennium. He waited for a lull in the discussion, and then remarked, with that decisive authority which always has characterized the class,

'I can settle the point at issue in a moment. All the old men were on one side and all the young men were on the other. There was, indeed, a difference in favour of the old politicians of one hundred and twenty-two years, seven months and a day.'

'But the young politicians were probably right,' interposed Jonathan.

'Might I be favoured with the reason for that profound observation?' sneeringly queried Sir William.

'With pleasure,' replied Jonathan. 'The young politicians are probably right because they are probably not politicians.'

Shrugging his shoulders so as to indicate as supreme a contempt as was compatible with good breeding, the patron turned to a less epigrammatic and more congenial guest, and proceeded to a scientific investigation of the national misfortunes. So far the evening had only enlightened Prior as to Jonathan's position in Moor Park, and very heartily sorry for St. John's friend he felt. But for that night he never could have fully appreciated how the proud spirit writhed under the shafts of contemptuous arrogance, or have understood the agony of Jonathan Swift at the mercy of Sir William Temple! Thus much Prior gathered very early from what he saw, and gathered it all the more certainly because the gaunt secretary, in refusing to make sport for the Philistines was clearly, as his master's polite astonishment indicated, doing a very unusual thing.

An episode occurred before long which showed Prior how deeply the venom had eaten into the great, sombre soul.

As the evening wore on, one or two of

the company succumbed more or less to the insidious influence of good cheer in a way which two hundred years ago was polite and ordinary. Sir William, who hated excess of any kind, always endeavoured to tear his guests away from the polished mahogany and bright decanters directly any signs of undue spirits manifested themselves, but, of course, with a success which was inversely proportional to the necessity. On the occasion in question he had made more than one abortive attempt to deliver the Earl of Soimême from temptation; but the earl would not be delivered, drank like a fish, and passed through the various stages between sobriety and what is technically known in our modern police courts as 'quarrelsome drunk.' Once there, the latent animosity against poor Swift blazed out.

'A glass of wine with you, Mr. Swift.'

With a bow and a conventional acknowledgment Jonathan raised his glass to his lips and put it down again.

'I suppose the wine is not so good as you are accustomed to when you are at home,' remarked the noble lord, with an offensive chuckle, 'or you would drink a glass when civilly asked to do so, eh ?'

Jonathan had not been taking the least notice for some time of his old antagonist, and did not at once do him the justice to suppose he was intoxicated; so, instead of taking no notice of the vulgar boor, he replied quietly, as though he were stating a simple fact of neither interest nor con-sequence,

'I have no home beyond that which Sir William kindly affords me.'

'Poor devil,' grinned the peer, seeing a glimmer of what he mistook for wit some-where in the distance. 'Your kingdom is not of this world, eh? But come now, you are going to be a parson—take care of the next one.'

No answer beyond a look of intense withering scorn.

'Ah, I see. I had forgotten the fees certainly *are* heavy. Come, gentlemen,' he cried, helping himself on to his legs with difficulty, 'let us assist suffering merit, and make a collection for Mr. Swift's fees.'

Jonathan looked down the table at Sir William, and he, in turn, stared fixedly at his glass. Then Jonathan rose, and left the room. So did Prior, and, to his honour be it spoken, so did Mr. Sawder, who had been keeping himself out of harm's way during the evening by the talisman of silence. Then Sir William, seeing that his secretary was not altogether unsupported, diplomatically rose too, as though to complete the festivities; and the party adjourned. Prior got hold of Jonathan in the passage, and whispered, indignantly,

'I should challenge him, or his son, or somebody, if I were you. The heartless, brutal, contemptible, empty-headed blackguard !'

'That is just why I shall ignore him,' answered Swift. 'He is what he is. Would you have me challenge my species ? Shall I fight him for being a man ?'

Prior shivered. That was a terrible thing to be said in such quiet, terrible earnest.

CHAPTER XIV.

NEXT day Prior returned to London with his official letters and an unofficial, or, in other words, a deep and real pity for the dark, sombre secretary, with the haggard, care-worn face, and lip on which a bitter curl was gradually becoming habitual.

'Worst of all,' thought he, 'is the desperate effort to fight his sorrow—to be himself—to drown care in forced gaiety. It is like jokes on a death-bed.'

And so the thought of whether anything could be done for 'Swift, poor fellow,' and, if so, what? was constantly present to his mind during his drive to

London. Once there, and free of his work, he betook himself to Henry St. John for advice and assistance. St. John was deep in the preparation of a great speech. Few people, now-a-days, prepare great speeches, but then, few people, now-a-days, make great speeches. That is probably because the modern standard of oratory is, like the standard for recruits, one of length. Beauty and sense in both cases are secondary considerations—if that. Poor Lord Palmerston. Nobody in his senses ever thought him an orator; but he was too good to be praised at a civic dinner by the man who was once right, because 'he spoke for four hours and twenty minutes, from the close of one day to the dawning of the next.'

So St. John greeted his friend with a laughing 'You execrable old worry, go away. I don't know this wretched concern any means by heart yet, and I am no better hand at impromptu composition than are my betters. The ideas come more readily during debate than at any other time, but the clothing——— Now, go away, there's a good fellow, go away, and spend to-morrow with me instead.'

'Can't,' answered Prior, 'the speech might be too much for you. You might break the appointment; besides, the question is serious. Your old friend Swift is in a very bad way. I like him. He is clever. He said something I hadn't heard before. Naturally, too, he is a good-hearted, generous fellow. I don't believe that, till misfortune and trouble drove him to it, he was the least like his present self—a bitter, cynical disbeliever in the very capacity of human nature for good.'

'Come, he isn't that now,' interposed St. John.

'Yes, he is. His very appearance has

changed greatly since the terrible affair at Merton. For that, I can vouch. As to his mind, of course I did not know him then, but still, I dare swear, it has changed fully as much as his face. There are indications enough and to spare that his intensely warped views of men and actions are the product of circumstances, and are far from innate. However, the fact remains, however it got there; and I am very deeply concerned. Swift is not a man with whom one can associate for ten minutes without feeling his supremacy over the herd; and, remember, for that very reason, if the dark view of life becomes *too* dark, he is sure to take one of two courses.'

'Eh?' queried St. John. 'Commit suicide, or, if he have too much principle for that—go mad! Good God! it is not so bad as that, surely?'

'It is rapidly becoming so.'

'Poor fellow! poor fellow! Tell me, what must I do?'

'That is precisely what I don't know,' answered Prior; 'but you should certainly do something if you can: I won't insult your sterling heart by saying if you wish. My own feeling is that Moor Park will kill him. Shut up there, his gigantic talents perfectly unrecognised, snubbed, bullied, insulted—and he as proud as Lucifer— and regarding Sir William, as it seemed to me, with a quiet contempt, mingled to some extent with a personal animosity which I cannot explain, and yet kicked by him, forced to crouch to him—why, I believe, St. John, I should go mad myself.'

'Is all this disappointed ambition, do you think?' asked St. John.

And then Prior answered, as the world has answered, how wrongfully you know now, reader, to some extent,

'Yes, I suppose that is how to put it,

though it does not seem a kind way. Listen: there was a dinner at Moor Park, and a whole lot of gentry, &c., &c., came. Not one of them was fit intellectually to be dust beneath Swift's boots. Well, they despised him utterly, and they showed it. A lion *can* be stung to death by gnats, St. John.'

We know that Prior was but very partially right as yet. Jonathan had failed, and failure had soured him as only failure so utterly unmerited could; but that was only one side in the prism through which men seemed Yahoos.

'Look you, Matt, this is very much my fault. I was piqued a bit, I confess, at the half-churlish way in which Swift received my condolences and offers of friendly assistance after that terrible night at Merton. It was very contemptible of me to be so unjust, but I pettishly let him alone for a long time, and when I thought better of it and wrote to him, his reply very naturally was not encouraging.'

'Oh, come,' said Prior, 'in all conscience there is nothing to blame you about—it is none of your business.'

'What, to be my brother's keeper? Yes, if I reasonably can. Lord Capel is going down somewhere or other in that part of the world to-day. I will get him to give me a lift so far for company, and then post on to Moor Park, and see what can be done.'

'But the debate, the speech!'

'Bother them both; there will be lots more chances. I have all my life to make a reputation in, but the odds are against my ever having the opportunity again of saving a Jonathan Swift from the alternative of suicide or madness.'

CHAPTER XV.

I occasionally apologise for digressing too much. I believe I ought rather to apologise for not digressing enough—as, for instance, this chapter is a direct continuation of the last one, which is amazing in a biography. Besides, there are not twenty-seven dozen people introduced who have nothing whatever to do with my hero or his fate. This also is amazing in a biography. I can only beg pardon generally once for all, and proceed.

While St. John was on his way to Moor Park, Jonathan was engaged in quarrelling outright with Sir William. That worthy personage had been excessively irritated by his secretary's assumption of perfect equality, or more, with the remaining guests at the big dinner. True, Sir William always made a point of maintaining in its strictest entirety this position himself, and, moreover, he considered that his private secretary was in mere virtue of his post a person of considerable consequence. On this theory Jonathan had acted, and Sir William was profoundly annoyed.

There were circumstances, too, which tended to intensify this sense of annoyance. Ever since Jonathan had been deputed to convey Sir William's views about the Triennial Bill to the king, and had fairly been installed in the post he occupied, instead of being a mere hanger-on, Sir William had treated him with the strictest possible regard of the laws of etiquette. There had been no more buttery dinners and no more suggestions about recruiting, and the great man considered himself entitled to the little one's gratitude for concessions so considerable. For some time Jonathan's apathetic indifference had served instead. He had not crouched, but he had not troubled himself to rise. From the day, however, when the conviction was forced upon him that Sir William was as despicable in morals as he was ordinary in mind, Jonathan's conduct, as I have already pointed out, changed entirely. So Sir William's annoyance at our hero's self-defence was deepened by a conviction of his ingratitude and his abuse of his benefactor's extraordinary kindness. The upshot of all this was an interview pretty much as follows:

'Good morning, Mr. Swift.'

'Good morning, Sir William.'

'Were you under the impression Lord Soimême was "lord" by courtesy?'

'Oh, dear no, that is the very *last* thing I should ever have imagined. He is a peer in his own right, isn't he?'

'It certainly surprises me to hear you say so,' returned Sir William. 'Your remarks were not such as a peer of the realm ought to be subjected to.'

'I cordially agree with you,' answered Jonathan. 'Isn't it sad he deserved them?'

'If you remember in future, Mr. Swift, the fundamental principle of English jurisprudence when you are tempted to fly at such high game, it may be of advantage to you.'

'Ah, you mean trial by his peers. Then he will get off scot free; for I don't insult human nature by supposing it possible to empanel a jury of his peers. By the way, it is a small matter, and I beg your pardon for calling your attention to it, but it certainly seems to me that, after Lord

Soimême had insulted **me** publicly, you should, in strict courtesy, have summoned your footman, and turned him out of doors.'

'Ah! that is your opinion.'

'It was, **until** you sneered. **You see, a** sneer is such an exceedingly cogent argument.

'Mr. Swift!'

'Sir William!'

Then a pause followed, which the baronet broke **by** saying,

'If you object to my conduct, the remedy is in your own hands. At the same time, I confess you **do** your work well, and your resignation would inconvenience me. **All** I have **to** object to is your flippantly, contemptuously caustic manner: but to that I *do* object **most strongly.**'

Then rising, **he left** the room, **and** allowed Jonathan **to** meditate on **the** crushing power **of** repartee that **man** wields who **pays one's** wages.

Very shortly after this interview, which Sir William had judiciously postponed until some days after the dinner which gave rise to it, Henry St. John arrived at Moor Park on his apparently Quixotic errand of mercy. The same afternoon Sir William had, again judiciously, gone away on a visit to an old comrade in state-craft, who lived five and thirty miles away, hoping thereby to leave his secretary time for consideration.

'Efficient secretaries are not too easily found,' he thought. 'It would be a nuisance, if the fellow took me at my word, and resigned, more especially if the reprimand does him good.'

So St. John found Moor Park masterless, and was at liberty to devote himself exclusively to the object of his visit. He saw at a glance that Prior had not exaggerated the painful state of mind into which poor Jonathan had drifted, and shuddered to think how near his friend

was to the terrible 'alternative.' It was
with great difficulty that he dragged Swift
into conversation sufficiently unembar-
rassed to indicate the whole depth of his
disease and misery, but he stuck manfully
to his guns, and obtained his wish at last.
What pained him most was the chill which
had come over Jonathan's old enthusiasm
for the grand and noble. It seemed altogether gone, vanished, dissipated. Once
especially this struck him. He had been
talking of his own career as an easy way
of indirectly finding out if Jonathan had
any of his old hopes and ambitions left,
the realization of which would please him,
and he incidentally mentioned a debate in
which he had taken part, and the subject
of which was the limitation of the regal
authority.

'They were sneering,' said St. John,
'at Divine Right, but I told them there is
no right which is not Divine.'

He looked in vain for the old gleam to brighten the sombre face with pleasure at the great truth put so forcibly. It grew darker, rather, and the reply came bitterly.

'They have hatched the devil since that was true!'

It presently appeared, however, that there was one subject in which Jonathan took as much interest as ever. St. John happened to apologise for a default of news which, as coming straight from the metropolis, he might have been expected to impart.

'The fact is,' he remarked, 'everything has been so quiet that there is no news.'

'The balance of power is restored, then, with a vengeance,' answered Jonathan. 'What, is nobody's wickedness uppermost?'

'Come, now, this is too bad. A week ago—I had forgotten—the foundations were laid of a new hospital, a gigantic place. Whose wickedness was that?'

'I don't know. Whose good is it? I will make an exception in his favour if he be alive.' '

St. John had to confess it was the product of testamentary benevolence.

'Ah,' said Jonathan, 'when a man takes a start like that of his good deeds, they come after him certainly, but I very much doubt their ever catching him. Never mind, let the founder alone, and tell me all about the hospital. Who is it for?'

'Anybody who needs it, and for whom there is room,' answered St. John, who forthwith found himself landed in the middle of an animated discussion upon the most efficient means of administering such institutions for the benefit of the suffering and distressed. This was a clue, and he followed it up.

'You seem to take a vast deal of interest in this hospital question,' he said at length.

'How can I help it?' was the answer. 'I should be a barbarian, a brute, a worse than I am, did I not. Is it not divine to be beneficent? Is it not—yes, in spite of the vice, evil, despicableness, which seem to be universal—is it not human?'

'True, old fellow; I am quite at one with you, though perhaps we may not agree as to the line of attack. Now I should waste myself as a philanthropic doctor, and am certainly not cut out for a parson, but in Parliament I may indirectly do as much good as either.'

'I agree with you fully,' replied Jonathan; 'you may very possibly do ten times as much.'

'But I should think,' boldly pursued his friend, 'that, holding the opinions you do, Moor Park is not exactly the groove in which Providence intended you to be hidden for any length of time. Why don't you take holy orders, and fling yourself heart and soul into the work you love?'

'Why? Because I can't afford it. I do not mind saying so to you, for you are a gentleman. But, do you know, Lord Soimême dined here with a large company the other day and asked me the question —in a very different manner, certainly— you have just asked. He answered it himself, too, just as I have, and then solved the difficulty by suggesting that a hat should be sent round on my behalf.'

'It is fortunate Sir William has not lost his best friend.'

'He has not lost any. He saw nothing peculiar in such conduct, and therefore did not resent it.'

'Oh!'

After a pause, during which he was deciding on the best way to put it, St. John resumed the thread of his idea.

'The expenses are very trifling. I know a Jew fellow who would find the ways and means for a good round rate of interest, if you assured the repayment against the income of your first living. Do forgive me for meddling with your private affairs in this way.'

'You are very kind,' answered Jonathan, fairly touched by the obvious sincerity of his friend's manner. 'No, it is not that I mean. The mere taking orders would cost scarcely anything, but I hold it disgraceful for a clergyman to be a pauper—not to himself, but to those who permit it,—and, therefore, no one should enter upon such a career until he knows the church has work for him to do which entitles the labourer to his hire.'

'Well, then, this is a case in point, if you are prepared for some self-sacrifice. There is an abominable place in Ireland called Kilroot. Do you know it? I don't. It is in the diocese of Connor, a district about which I am almost equally ignorant.

Lord Capel, who is **over here just** now—the lord-deputy, **you know**—mentioned to me that **the** prebend of Kilroot was **vacant.** It is worth **next to** nothing, **only a** hundred **a year, and** the place is so **vile it is a** struggle **to catch a** parson who will live there. **By** the **way,** there **is** plenty **of work to be done.** The degradation, **destitution, suffering, and villainy of** the people are unequalled.'

'Nay,' said Jonathan, '**don't** pretend **to** laugh at such things. Thank you, St. John, from the bottom of my heart for the delicate way **you** have put it. I am not ashamed to be indebted **to you. If you** can make Lord Capel give me **this** prebend, **I shall be** proud **to be obliged to** you, indeed I shall.'

CHAPTER XVI.

St. John forthwith changed the subject; he had gained his point, and saw his way to engraft on Jonathan's life the change of scene and circumstance which he believed was absolutely necessary as an antidote to the morbid turn events had given to his mind. And, that gained, he was too wise to lay himself open to the possibility of a counter-march; so he changed, as I say, the subject and asked, laughingly,

'What has become of the brown beauty?'

The look of pleased animation on Jonathan's face, that look which was so unusual **now, faded away** before **the** question.

‘You mean Miss Johnson?’

‘Yes.’

‘Oh, she does not live here **now.** A lady took Manor Cottage, and Miss **John-** son lives with her.’

‘Hullo! Who’s **the lady?’**

‘Mrs. Dingley.’

‘Nice?’

‘Very.’

‘On a footing of equality?’

‘I am not in a position to say. Appar- ently **yes.’**

‘Come,’ said St. John, ‘you must **take** me **over** this afternoon and introduce me formally. You know them, or at any rate her, well enough for that, don’t you?’

St. John clearly showed by his manner that **he** wished to go, and Jonathan did **not see his way** to an excuse consistent at once with veracity and his secret, so he reluctantly consented. And now, gentle reader, by your distinguished leave—having pointed out that this visit was far from being of Jonathan Swift's own seeking—I will proceed at once and shortly to record the story of it. Mrs. Dingley and Miss Johnson were at home, the servant said, but she was not sure whether they were not engaged. Being young and foolish, and a country girl to boot, she blushed forthwith and looked guilty.

'Who said so?' asked St. John.

'The parson, sir,' answered she.

'Then,' put in Jonathan, 'take in my name, and find out.'

It was odd that this suspicious ecclesiastic should want a private interview by back-stairs influence with the girl he doubted.

'Who? What parson?' asked St. John.

'A biped—five feet ten longitudinally, thirty-six inches round,' replied Jonathan, in a tone which told its own tale to the almost womanishly observant nature of his friend.

In a moment the servant came back to usher them in, and Mr. Sawder had bestowed his shilling in vain. The two ladies and the 'biped' looked anything but confidential, to say the least of it, as Jonathan entered the room ; but St. John noticed that Stella, uninterested as she had looked till then, seemed to brighten in the presence of the ugly secretary.

'This is interesting,' he thought. 'I should like exceedingly to know what it all means.'

Jonathan devoted himself almost exclusively to Mrs. Dingley, leaving his friend and Stella to spar to their hearts' content. Mr. Sawder discerned the change in the situation which the new visitors had brought about, and was, reasonably enough, very much out of humour. Nobody likes to feel that his efforts to make himself agreeable have resulted in weariness of the flesh. So Mr. Sawder lay in wait, metaphorically speaking, for opportunities of asserting himself and his superiority, as common-place men always do under the circumstances, very generally at considerable costs and charges to themselves.

'You must talk politics to Mr. St. John, Stella, if you want to interest him in the remotest degree,' laughed Mrs. Dingley, 'mustn't she, Mr. Swift?'

'Accuse him of that, if you can, when I have told you this,' stoutly returned Jonathan; and he repeated St. John's aphorism,

"There is no right which is not divine."

Was he who said that a member of Parliament or a man?'

'Ha! ha! ha!' laughed Mr. Sawder, forcing a laugh to begin with, as was his wont at such times, much as a fusilade precedes a bayonet charge. 'Ha! ha! ha!

then Henry VIII. married six wives by divine right.'

'The assumption being,' remarked Stella, 'that right and **wrong are convertible** terms; but that, you know, is not generally admitted.'

'Mr. Sawder,' put in Jonathan, patronizingly, 'is probably referring to the theory of government known as "Divine Right," forgetting for the moment that that theory **was** unknown in the **time of** Henry VIII., and that, moreover, Henry was the son of a conqueror.'

Mr. Sawder was settled for the time being, and **the** conversation rolled **over** him again.

'Well, **then,**' asked Stella, '*may* I talk politics ?'

'Certainly, if you won't ask puzzling questions, expose my ignorance, and then laugh at me,' answered St. John.

'Very well, when **I** expose your ignorance, I promise to weep over it. Question one. How do you like the government, barring always our sovereign lord the king?'

'Answer one. If I liked them, it would be by an effort, but I don't. The king is a king, the ministers are head clerks, with memorandum-books superadded, and the one idea of the whole job lot is to govern a great nation by the system of double entry.'

'Or, to be flippant, don't you think they would rather stay in for ever than get in twice?'

'Nay,' said St. John, 'be flippant about anything in the world but this. Consider how vast the destinies of this great country if those who are entrusted with the direction of affairs but recognize and accept them. Consider the mighty influence on civilization England might exert, an influence ever growing and widening, deepening with the channel in which it ran, if these "statesmen" would not thrust opportunity aside and turn their backs on Providence. But they prefer rather to be the ministers of a shop than the directors of a mighty engine of philanthropy and beneficence. It needs no prophet to foretell that England will one day stand at the helm of God's great purpose, steering by the star of right to the infinitely glorious goal of peace on earth and goodwill towards men, for—— She might do so now, if she chose; and can one conceive of such a mighty power given absolutely in vain?'

'But how long will she stand there?'

'Just so long as she can appreciate a higher, a nobler mission than her own material prosperity. Just so long as the star by which she guides humanity is not obscured, hidden, lost for ever beneath the murky haze of twopence on the funds and

cries for cheap taxation. Just so long as
the good of her own people within her
own shores is *not* the leading aim of her
existence. Just so long as a spirit of
Divine self-sacrifice animates her statesmen and her people, and leads them to see
in all their privileges, in all their opportunities, not so much to live upon but so
much to do.'

He said all this with animation, and yet
so low that Jonathan could just overhear
him. St. John by the way had probably
the finest voice, and the voice most perfectly under command, of any orator of
the age in which he lived. Then the
answer came.

'Mr. St. John, you are right; heartily,
earnestly I agree with you, and I do so
wish more people were of your mind.'

'Ah,' he answered, 'you have a conscience then ;'—and laughing—' excuse

my surprise, **but** ladies so rarely have consciences.'

Jonathan heard this too, and looked for some quiver to betray that the unmeant sarcasm had **cut.** But no, there **was no** ghost of such a thing. The clear, **dark eyes smiled** a quiet incredulity **at the general** proposition, **and,** catching Jonathan's **glance,** their **owner** asked, **in** tones which, if counterfeit, left truth and falsehood henceforward indistinguishable by mortal man,

'Do you hear what **Mr.** St. John says about ladies, Mr. Swift? You could have given me **a** character for **conscience,** couldn't **you?**'

'**It** depends on one's turn of **mind,**' was the reply. '**You** see, **some** people look out for **the rule** and others for the exception. If my intelligence had been of the former **class, I** should never have **found you out.**'

'Come, come,' interposed Mr. Sawder, 'I claim a wider experience than either of you two gentlemen, and I maintain that ladies have, ninety-nine times out of a hundred, a keener sense of right and wrong than have men.'

Then he looked with admiring, submissive unction at Stella, and Jonathan, noticing the glance, wondered at its compatibility with Mr. Sawder's profession of grave doubt.

During the afternoon the same wonder was excited more than once. Mr. Sawder was to all appearance worshipping at the shrine he reviled, not obtrusively nor remarkably, but still worshipping beyond all question. Even Jonathan, who was not generally of at all an observant disposition, could see so much as that, and St. John noticed another thing into the bargain which puzzled him intensely. It was this: Jonathan on two occasions left the room with Mrs. Dingley to advise her about some flowers in the porch, and each time, while he was absent from the room, Mr. Sawder's attentions to Stella Johnson were redoubled, rose, as it were, to the flood. Presently the little party broke up, and, directly they started for Moor Park, St. John broke forth into praise of Stella—her beauty, wit, good nature, everything, and, turning suddenly upon his friend at the close of his rhapsody, he said,

'Jonathan, that woman loves you, and loves you as only such a woman could love.'

'Did she tell you so?' sneered Swift.

'Yes, if a man is more than the antithesis of a deaf mute.'

'Certainly, St. John, you put things in a very epigrammatic and forcible way,' said Jonathan, in the desperate hope of changing the subject. But his friend was not to be so easily diverted from his purpose.

'Snub me if you like,' he said, 'tell me I have nothing in the world to do with it, and that I am impertinent to ask, but nevertheless I *do* ask, are you going to ignore the love you have inspired in a goddess like that?   Nonsense!—it is impossible.'

'Why don't you marry her yourself if you admire her so?' was the evasive answer—an answer which next moment Jonathan would have given worlds to recall.

Suppose such a contingency did arise as that he had hinted at!   This man was his friend, his benefactor; his sacred duty would be to tell him what there was to fear.   The hideous idea chilled him to the bone.   He, who loved her so intensely, so desperately, with caught breath, as it were, until *certainty* should come to change the love to hatred—*he* to be the publisher of her shame! It was too much. Involuntarily he stopped abruptly, as though to steady himself.

'Are you ill?' asked St. John, alarmed by the pale ashy face, the dead cold hand, and the big beads of perspiration on the brow. But it was over in a moment.

'Yes, momentarily—my heart, I think —I am better now.' And then, manfully trying to avert suspicion, Jonathan recurred to the subject by asking what his friend thought of the Rev. Mr. Sawder.

'Why, broadly speaking, I hate him. He would be better if he were a bad man, but I don't think he is. He is a conscientious sinner, and is wicked by inadvertence. He is passionately in love with Stella, and abominates you because he fancies you are a rival. You noticed how he spooned, didn't you?' A nod for answer. 'Well, it was ten times worse when you left the room; it became distinctly pronounced. Why should he object to your hearing his neat-turned compliments?'

'Ah, was that so?' asked Jonathan, with some surprise. 'Perhaps he feared I might retail them myself. Well, here we are at the Dutch boat-house, and now for a quiet evening and a glass of Burgundy.'

But, in spite of the Burgundy, Jonathan was very poor company that night. Mr. Sawder had first given definite shape to his suspicions. Could it be Mr. Sawder had discovered he was wrong? And how quietly innocent Stella looked when St. John had mentioned conscience as he did! Could she—but no, and, remembering the laurel-bush, he hardened his heart. Alas! poor Jonathan!

CHAPTER XVII.

'COME at once. Jimmy is dying. **In** his delirium **he** asks for you. Your presence may quiet the poor little **boy.** His mother's agony is terrible.'

It was a note from Stella, written in pencil from the bedside of the little patient so fast nearing the end. Jonathan ran for his hat without an instant's hesitation, although he had firmly resolved not to meet Stella again, save for the short good-bye society ordained before he sailed for Ireland. There was no thought of his own feelings left, however, in face **of the note. If** his presence could soothe the poor wastrel, come home to him what pain there might, he would not stay away. Overruling Providence was about to give him one more chance of discovering the grossness of his error while there was yet time, one more opportunity of seeing, if he had eyes to see, and did not wilfully blind himself to the evidence his soul was yearning to receive, that the stars themselves were not more pure than their namesake.

Only a dull moaning was to be heard when Jonathan entered the cottage where the boy whom he had reprieved for so short a time lay dying. It was the mother who was moaning. Seated on a stool away altogether from the bed, she rocked restlessly to and fro, moaning her misery. The boy was apparently sleeping, and Stella, standing by the bed, was holding his wasted hand in hers. Jonathan saw that the end was very near. Medical skill and kindness could do no more now but watch for the few grains to run in the hour-glass, the last dull spark of the taper to be quenched. And looking at the pinched white features, the lines of care and suffering on the face where time had hardly begun to write, Jonathan felt that perhaps so far as the little sufferer were concerned it was better even here that death should come. But the mother!

'Why does she give way so? It seems more than ordinary grief,' he whispered to Stella.

Stella shook her head. Just then Jimmy opened his eyes, and, seeing Jonathan standing by, he smiled a sweet, sad little smile, and tried to speak. But strength was ebbing, and the moving lips gave no utterance. They poured some cordial down his throat and listened. But the eyes had wandered to Stella now, and the only sound that reached their ears was 'sing.' And Stella, mastering her feelings, sang to him a childish hymn of his Redeemer and the home to which he was going ; sang it with earnest reverence as in the presence of the Great White Throne, with her cheeks pale with emotion and her eyes full of tears ; sang it low and tremulously, but, oh ! so sweetly, and the boy seemed comforted and smiled again. And his mother heard the hymn and crept back nearer to the bed. Jonathan moved a little so as to let her take her mother's place if she would, but she shrank back only muttering, 'Not yet.'

But when the hymn was finished she started and asked, with awful intenseness,

'Sing it again ! Sing it again, for God's sake ! *Perhaps* He will hear you !'

So Stella sang another verse or two. But the end was almost come. Jimmy raised himself in bed, his face bathed in the light of dawning heaven, and said 'Mother.' Then all was over, but he had gone to sleep on his mother's breast. For a few moments there was a dead silence. The broken-hearted parent was too stunned to realize at once that the dreaded time had come. At last she laid her burden down and stood gazing as in a dream, while Jonathan reverently closed the little sleeper's eyes never to open again until time shall be merged in eternity. The action seemed to rouse the mother from her trance, and a look of anguish such as no tongue could utter and no pen can describe came upon her face.

'Suffer the little children to come unto me, and forbid them not, for of such is the Kingdom of Heaven,' said Jonathan, trusting to the balm of Gilead to bring its infallible relief.

But as from outer darkness came the moan,

'Take my soul, my God, in ransom for his. The sin was mine. Let *me* suffer; not my boy, my baby.'

Then she fell on the pale face, radiant with that strange light, crying passionately,

'My darling, oh, my darling! oh, come back!'

Jonathan looked inquiringly at Stella; there was more here, he could see, than ordinary grief; and while the paroxysm lasted he whispered, gently,

'What is it? She seems to have more than lost him!'

Still Stella shook her head, but his own question had enlightened Jonathan. It flashed across him, as he spoke, that Mrs. Grey was a papist and that her boy had never been baptised. Did she fear she had lost him for ever?

'Look,' he said to her, gently, when

exhausted **nature brought a** lull in the storm of grief. ' Look, **you** can *see* he has gone to heaven.'

' Impossible, impossible,' she cried. ' **He** had all his **sins upon him.** He has died in them. Oh, God! Oh, God!!'

Then Jonathan tried kindly and winningly **to** assure her **how** wrong she **was,** and to point out how infinitely broader were the grounds of our hope than priesthoods or than ceremonies. **But** all in **vain.** The wretched mother refused **to be** comforted, and kept moaning again **and** again,

' He was born in sin, and he has died in sin.'

Presently Jonathan desisted in despair, and then Stella took the desolate woman's hand, knelt beside her, and poured in her **ear** all the **comfort of** a sister's sorrow. Jonathan instinctively withdrew a little, as though feeling that there should be no more spectators of such a scene. In spite of himself, however, he *did* watch the kneeling form and upturned face with intense earnestness. Stella looked far, far more than beautiful, just then she looked angelic. Some of the radiance from the tiny dead face seemed reflected through her tears, and some of the music from the celestial choirs welcoming the little soul seemed to sound in the tones of her pleading voice as she urged the mercy of his and her Redeemer.

Look, Jonathan, look, drink it in. You are a theologian, and you remember the argument that, if Jesus Christ were not God's incarnate, He must have been the worst of men. Remember it, think, look. Is this the ghastly sham of an abandoned woman? Is this the hideous mockery of a contradicted life? Is this an awful blasphemy in the presence of Death, and sor-

row which is worse than death itself?
Do you think so? Dare you think so?
Then fly from her this instant, for she
must be a devil indeed!

CHAPTER XVIII.

NEVERTHELESS, two or three days afterwards Jonathan walked over to bid a for-
mal good-bye to Mrs. Dingley and her
'companion' prior to leaving Moor Park,
as he believed, and tried to hope, for ever.
The interview was soon over. Very ordinary indeed too, it was, on the face of it.
No one would have suspected that Stella
was going upstairs to cry directly the
door closed behind her visitor, nor that
Jonathan, as he turned away with a conventional compliment, was utterly desolate.
On that, however, I need not dwell yet.

Jonathan had, in face of circumstances

which ought to **have carried** happy conviction to his mind, persisted in his doubts. **Let** us see what came of it. **Under no** circumstances, probably, would **he have** refused St. John's proposal, enabling him as **it** did to realize **his** life-long **wish of** entering the **church ; but the** spirit **in** which **he would have** entered **on his new** work **and** the tone of his mind and temper would have been very different had not this shadow clouded and enshrouded **him.** Pray recall one moment, gentle reader, what it was that Jonathan Swift had suffered.

Endowed by Providence with stupendous genius, intensely sensitive **feelings,** and a great ambition **to be the** benefactor of his species, **and, if** might be, to be remembered as **such, Fate** had thwarted him at every turn. He had been driven by poverty from the university. **He had** risked all upon his literary **prowess, and** had twice failed utterly, while the mother and the sister whom he loved so well were almost starving through his failure. The world had done its best to make him hate his fellows, had soured him, had striven to crush him; then he had given in, and taken nobly to drudgery for the sake of his dear ones, putting up almost cheerfully with the galling impertinence of Moor Park littleness for the holy purpose of earning his mother's living. Then he lost these dear ones, worse than lost them—he found he had mistrusted them. And then this girl whom he loved—bad too. What wonder that he was beginning to find it easy, whether 'terrible and devilish' or no, to hate! hate! hate! A sad frame of mind for anybody, but saddest of all for a clergyman, whose mission it is to preach a Gospel of Love.

Perhaps it was this which accounted for Jonathan's failure in the work he now undertook; for fail he did, in spite of all his efforts—and most conscientiously persevering those efforts were. Lord Capel presented him with his prebend with so little delay that within a few weeks of leaving Moor Park Jonathan was fairly settled at Kilroot, living well within his income of a hundred a year, and distributing the surplus in alms which seemed never to promote anything but the liquor traffic. The district was a very poor one, and the inhabitants as ignorant, callous, and debased as was consistent with their remaining human, or even Irish.

To make them think about this life would have been a triumph, to impress upon their attention the importance of the next a miracle. Yet we know that even in such places as was this, and among people such as these, great works of infinite consequence have been done again and again by men compared with whom Jonathan Swift was a demi-god. Still the fact remains that he could not do it. There was no want of compassion on his part. His heart was as tender in presence of human woe as it had ever been, but sympathy in its correct, restricted sense was wanting. No effort would bring that back. If you look upon mankind as Yahoos, you may compassionate them but you cannot sympathise with them; it is impossible. And without that sympathy there is very little good done, even to the cultured, while with the ignorant and degraded it is the only handle which philanthropy can grasp, the only sense to which it can appeal. So the months and weeks rolled by, bringing each one the conviction more closely home to Jonathan that his life was being wasted and that his mission was a failure. This far from cheering thought was Jonathan's constant companion when he gave himself time to think at all, and it helped to make

the musings of his uncurbed mind more
bitter than ever. To shut reflection out as
much as possible he had no resource but
reading, for society there was none that
was congenial to him. So he read, or
rather studied, morning, noon, and night,
every instant that his parochial duties left
him unemployed.

Even while walking from cottage to cot-
take, or rather hut to hut, a sheet with
notes upon St. Cyprian, St. Jerome, or
other of the fathers was always in his
hand. Before a year had elapsed this intense application bore its natural fruit in
a severe nervous attack, accompanied, of
course, by entire depression of the miserable
fragments of animal spirits poor Jonathan
had left. He was inundated by overpowering darkness, and assailed by all the
powers of evil that habited the memories
of the past. The misery was unbearable.
He flew back to his books and intensified

the evil for a moment's respite. At last one morning, after a sleepless night, spent indeed in poring over abstruse cogitations upon points of faith with all the intensity of fear, nature could bear the strain no longer, and *that* came once more. I will not describe it. I will not picture him. Only one thing left in all the wide, wide world—his mind—and mad! Oh, God, what agony. For weeks afterwards he was numbed, as it were, and torpid. The rack is an anæsthetic after a time. And when he came to himself again, thoroughly recognising his utter, his unutterable loneliness, not having even himself for a companion, he began to yearn with all the weary longing of a broken spirit for human kindness, or at least for pity. You may say it was weak and inconsistent to despise his race, as he was fast beginning to do, and yet to long for their love and sympathy. It was perhaps; but it was human certainly.

Such was Jonathan Swift after a little more than a year of the Kilroot life had passed over him, and, in such a frame of mind, can it be wondered at that his thoughts often reverted to the one living creature whose love would have chiefly solaced him, dared he have accepted it? A drowning man clutches at straws, they say, and it is certainly true morally, if not physically. Jonathan, feeling sorely crushed and wounded, panted for this loving sympathy he might not accept, and peered back at the shadows of the past to see if there was no opening through which light could come. I should point out here that Jonathan knew, with the unerring instinct of love, that Stella loved him. Down in the depths of his soul, that is to say, he was certain of it. Perhaps, if the question had been put to him, or if he had put it to himself, he would have more than hesitated to return a favourable answer.

But, to anyone who knows anything at all of the difference between faith and belief, I need not insist on the perfect compatibility of the intuition and the doubt. He knew by intuition, he doubted by reason. Or, more correctly speaking, he would have doubted, had circumstances led him to give definite shape to his vague, unfashioned yearnings. Will the gentle reader be so good as to pay especial attention to this apparently unimportant point; for a time was soon coming when this undercurrent of firm faith in Stella's love was to exercise a mighty influence on Jonathan's whole career.

One stormy night he sat listening to the howling wind and lashing rain. The storm was raging fearfully. He remembered only one as bad, that one which blew the stranger to his mother's door, that one which brought upon its cursed wings Lauriel's destroyer. And the thought came into his mind, 'Would to God there were left in the land of the living some one to tell me all, and I *might* not have to think so hardly of my poor little sister !'

As he thought, it dawned upon him like a revelation that he was praying for what, in the case of the woman he chiefly loved, he did not trouble to avail himself of, although the means were, at any rate possibly, within his reach. Would he some day repeat the petition, the necessity for which he had himself procured, for some one left to tell him not to remember poor dead Stella quite so hardly? There came a rap on his door, and his servant, entering, brought in a letter from Sir William Temple. It was the first Jonathan had had from his old master, as was natural enough, in view of the, to say the least of it, strained character of their mutual relations when they parted.

The letter was in strange coincidence with Jonathan's thoughts at the moment when it arrived, and it was with mixed feelings that he read as follows :—

' DEAR SIR,

'You are surely tired of Ireland by this time. St. John came to Moor Park some days ago, and told me your health was, he thought, suffering from the damp climate, and that you were, moreover, disappointed at your discovery that not even Christianity can make a human being out of an Irishman. If this is so, why do you not come back? It would, I confess, be a great convenience to me were you reinstalled in your old post. No one has at all filled your place, and my own health precludes my doing more than mere dilletante work. Of course I should not expect you to come back for ever, nor on the old terms; and

Lord Soimême is dead. Further, I can assure you that what influence I have shall be exerted to procure your promotion to some English cure where your talents will not be so hopelessly wasted as they must necessarily be in preaching to Irish peasants or their pigs.'

That was all I need quote, but there were many kindly expressions in what followed over which Jonathan smiled peculiarly. The letter had been long delayed by the stormy state of the Channel, and required, therefore, an immediate answer. Jonathan sat down to think what he should do. Certainly it was true his work was a failure, utter and complete, and all the will in the world would never qualify him to discharge his duties more efficaciously. Wherever he went, whatever he did, it was useless to stop here. And, if he left Kilroot, why should he not return to Moor Park? Certainly it was painful to him, under the circumstances, to be liable to meet poor Stella; but still there was a hope, and he felt passionately anxious to be once more within the reach of the beatific vision that the revelation of his error would afford his soul.

I daresay the nineteenth century gentlemen, who boast the morality of the present administration and the gentlemanly feeling of the Birmingham ' school,' will sneer at Jonathan Swift because he did not set his mind at rest once for all by interviewing Sir William Temple. But I am glad my hero is a real gentleman, who would not, to save himself all the agony of which his nature was capable, whisper even a question which implied suspicion of the woman he loved. Estimate *that*, oh political and other economists, in pounds and shillings and pence.

CHAPTER XIX.

So the result was that Jonathan returned to Moor Park, about a year after having quitted it, as he had expected and half hoped, for ever. He had learnt something in that year. He had discovered that human love is as necessary to the existence of a human being as are food and air. He had fathomed the depths of being absolutely alone, with no heart beating in unison with his, and without a soul who was sorry for him. There are men who can live like that years, decades; that is to say, there are men who are worse than a dead lion, to carry the illustration no further. Jonathan Swift found, as every *man* finds when the sad necessity for thinking at all about it arises, that solitary existence is a moral impossibility. All the intellectual faculties in the world are useless in face of feeling, for the heart is as much a component part of human nature as the mind. He knew this. He had learnt it. Before this year had elapsed, perhaps he might have questioned in his self-sufficiency the effect of loneliness upon *him*, and asserted that he, at least, could look upon the estrangement or aversion of all his species with sublime indifference. However, it was not so; experience had convinced him of that, and now I wish my readers, that they may understand this biography, to remember what a gigantic risk on this showing Jonathan was incurring when he returned to Moor Park. There was only one living soul to whom his sympathies went forth in what might be love, and that soul was Stella; and in coming back again to near her side he was staking his existence, as the man he was, on being able to lay hold on her affection as his last tie to humanity. Well, this is what came of it.

When Jonathan arrived at his old quarters, the first thing which struck him was the alteration in Sir William Temple. From being a fairly hale and hearty middle-aged man, the baronet seemed in twelve short months to have completely broken up. His very voice seemed altered. The commendatory ring was subdued and occasionally querulous, and the ' Ah, Mr. Swift!' that Jonathan remembered so well had sunk from a sneer to a plaint. The change was not altogether unexpected so far as Jonathan was concerned, for Sir William had been failing in a slight but unmistakable way for some little time; but still the first meeting under the altered circumstances shocked our hero very much. The bodily decay had evidently affected Sir William's power of will, while leaving his mind unimpaired, and that was precisely the province in which any alteration was the most remarkable.

'I am very glad to see you, Mr. Swift,' said the distinguished statesman, when they met—'very glad indeed. I want to get the better of that man Bentley, but somehow there is not energy enough left in me to stick to my work.'

Whereupon Jonathan thought, and very justly, that the constitution of Sir William —and all men like him—was certainly breaking up when they could not plod. Nevertheless, he was sorry. He would have hanged his employer with a keen sense of the righteousness of the deed (but for the benefit of his doubt); still as yet there was the doubt, and Jonathan

took advantage of it to be sorry for the
frail old man before him.

'You do not look at all well, Sir William.'

'No, I daresay not, and yet very possibly I look better than I am, Mr. Swift. I
am dying.'

'God forbid,' said Jonathan. 'And yet
I suppose, Sir William, that, as far as you
are concerned, you care exceedingly little
whether your life be longer or shorter?
You have employed your talents to the
best advantage for the world, and have
nothing'—looking straight at him—'to
regret.'

A smile, more cordial and less self-
asserting than of yore, was the only reply,
and the conversation was cut short by
the entrance of Sir William's physician,
and Jonathan withdrew. Downstairs, he
found Stella and Mrs. Dingley, who were

quite unaware of his arrival. Surprise at seeing him made Stella's pale face flush for a moment, but the colour soon faded again, and showed that the year gone by, had left its traces here too.

'You here, Mr. Swift!' said Mrs. Dingley. 'How soon you have tired of Ireland. Isn't there a proverb in the Bible or elsewhere about unstable as water?'

This was said with a feminine accentuation of bitterness, which clearly indicated a more or less personal interest in the accusation. Stella noticed the tone, and just the slightest possible colour rose in her sweet face again.

'Hadn't we better go home now?' she put in. 'The doctor may be a very long time upstairs, and you know I'm busy to-day.'

'Did you come to inquire after Sir William?' asked Jonathan.

'Yes.'

'He seems very ill indeed.'

Again 'Yes,' said with an effort at firmness.

'Nonsense; nothing of the kind,' interrupted Mrs. Dingley. 'A mere indisposition. He will be as well as ever in a week. Well, Mr. Swift, have you left Ireland for ever, or are you on a visit; and did you say good-bye to your friends when you took your departure?'

Whereupon Jonathan explained that he had resigned his prebend on the ground of ill health, and somewhat sadly added that he had no *friends* to whom to bid farewell.

'I suppose there is nobody in the world,' he said, 'more perfectly alone than am I.'

'That is generally a person's own fault,' stoutly rejoined Mrs. Dingley; but she was evidently mollified, nevertheless, by poor Jonathan's loneliness and his sense

of it—what woman would not have been?
—and added, 'Well, in default of more
agreeable company, you can come and see
us. We shall be glad to see you, sha'n't
we, Poppett?'

'Oh, certainly.'

A pause, while Jonathan considered that
the invitation could scarcely have been less
cordial; and then Stella, in dread of her
friend's mediatorial services, managed to
break off the conference. That night, Sir
William became much worse, and, being
for some hours in positive danger, a mes-
senger with the sad news was despatched
to Manor Cottage.

'Why on earth?' Jonathan asked himself; and indeed the world seemed beginning to wonder too, as a trifling incident
which occurred next day clearly enough
indicated. It was this. Two women-serv-
ants were dusting Jonathan's bed-room,
and, as he chanced to come leisurely along

the passage, he heard the one saying to the other,

'You don't like her, because, somehow, she is a lady, but you can't deny she is pretty.'

'That's right, sneer at my looks,' came the answer. 'You are not so very beautiful yourself, and, as for *Miss* Johnson, it might have been better for her to be ugly.'

At the time Jonathan heard these words he was going to his room to rest for an hour or two after a sleepless night spent at Sir William's bedside, but the humour left him on the instant.

'If everybody, from Sawder to Mary Jane doubts and whispers,' he muttered, half savagely, 'why, Truth must lie somewhere between Sawder and Mary Jane.'

The cloud was thickening. But I need not dwell on all this, further than to show that my hero, poor fellow, was rather to be praised for bearing up in spite of his temperament, and in spite of all the apparently good reasons to the contrary, than blamed for desponding so much as he did.

When I say 'bearing up,' I do hope I have made myself all through this biography distinctly understood. This was more than a mere matter of a passionate love. *That* it was certainly, and that it was under circumstances which rendered the issue peculiarly momentous, for it was all the love Jonathan Swift had left to bestow; but it was far more. Stella was in Jonathan's eyes an angel. If she were bad, he would never love again, and worse, if worse be possible, he never would believe again. Pause for a moment to consider how unutterably woeful that fate would be. Remember that in one sense disbelief annihilates for those who disbelieve the thing they disbelieve in. Remember, that it is possible to wipe, so far as oneself is concerned, a sponge across the grandest part of the great creation of God. Remember, that, though he may **reap** the tenderest solicitude, the generous profuseness **of the** most noble benevolence, **or the grand** heroism of the sublimest self-sacrifice, **still** to the man upon whom all this **is lavished, there** may be no such thing as **love,** no such thing as open-hearted generosity, no such thing as forgetfulness **of self.**

Come then, paint **me a fiend** and tell me how you would colour him! Would it not be **by** leaving out these things, by painting a man, **in** short, devoid of them? **And** now tell me further, can you conceive **of a** more stupendous desolation than he must suffer **who** while himself **among the nob-**lest and **best of** the sons **of men,** has been driven **or has** drifted **on the** rocks of such a miserable **scepticism?** Can you imagine a **more** unspeakable loneliness than **that** man would suffer? Can you even **dimly** picture one tithe of **his terrible** solitude?

That is why I say so much about this. The ordinary every-day passion of Mr. A. for Miss B. would certainly not have taken me so long. I would have left that as a prey for my dear friends the plodding historians, who would some day have found it and rejoiced greatly over adding one more fact of no importance whatever to the store of their learned ignorance.

To proceed, however, Sir William rallied wonderfully; the immediate danger passed away; Stella's visits and messages of inquiry became less and less frequent, and Jonathan returned, to some extent, to the old life and work.

CHAPTER XX.

JONATHAN noticed before many months
passed away that Henry St. John ran
down from town to see him oftener than
the circumstances seemed to warrant. A
line in Milton, a scrap in Ben Jonson, a
thought of Marlowe's, anything, everything
seemed to require a personal appeal to the
oracular secretariat at Moor Park. This
was flattering, and St. John was so agreeable as well as so brilliant, that it was also
very pleasurable; but Jonathan observed
more than this. He saw that St. John
would willingly remit Milton, Marlowe,
Jonson, the Angel Gabriel, or anything

else to the limbo of forgotten bores rather
than miss one moment of Hestor Johnson's company.   A call at Manor Cottage
ranked far above Macbeth or the Aglaura,
and a stroll round the scene of his discom-
fiture of a year before with the fair victor
seemed very much more entrancing than
any other employment whatsoever.   Jonathan knew too well what this meant.   It
meant that a time was coming when at
the supreme call of duty he would have to
blast the character of the woman he loved
to save his friend.   He would not do it to
save *himself*, not even would he breathe a
question in a whisper.   But, though he
would not do it for himself, he would for
duty, and, facing the probable contingency,
he waited quietly prepared in any case to
do what was right.   Facing day by day an
ordeal like this is not calculated to raise
even fairly buoyant spirits, and it had its
natural effect upon Jonathan.   Besides,

Sir William in his weak state of health was almost unable to give even the vague directions on the lines of which his secretary was in the habit of working, and so for weeks together Jonathan, with no work to do which must be done, had unlimited leisure to think.

So it came to pass that, during one of his perennial visits, St. John noticed that his friend was sinking into a state of mind verging on melancholy monomania, and at Manor Cottage the same evening he managed to have a talk with Stella about it.

'What on earth is to be done,' he asked her, 'with poor, dear Jonathan? As for me, I feel inclined to decline the combat any further. All my little efforts to save him from himself seem in vain. But it certainly seems hard to stand by and see so magnificent a man rendered useless to the world and worse than useless to himself, thanks to one unhappy twist in his humour : doesn't it ?'

'Very,' answered Stella, seriously. 'And, Mr. St. John, it is very good of you to care so much about it. I am sure that if Mr. Swift could get fairly hold of the idea that there are people in the world like you, and could see what you really are, it would do him all the good he needs.'

Stella said this very much in earnest, indeed so much so that she did not give a thought to the high compliment she was paying St. John. *He* did, however.

'It makes me happier than I can express that you should think of me thus.'

'Why ?' was the dexterous answer. 'I know, though poor Mr. Swift does not, that ninety-nine people out of a hundred are amiable and benevolent in reality, however apparently the reverse.'

'I wish I were the hundredth,' said St. John, a little crest-fallen, 'it would be better than being mixed up in a job lot even of all the virtues. I hate job lots. Well, since I am not to have my little compliment all to myself, let us return to business. What can I—or any other nine-tenths of human excellence do for poor Jonathan?'

'Help him to succeed,' said Stella. 'He has never yet known what that means. Success might electrify him out of the trance in which his better nature is lying. I believe it would.'

'Do you mean by success—reputation—a big bray?'

'Yes; you men like it, and very generally the greater you are (really are, I mean, the more you are above your fellows) the more you yearn for their commendation. The medicine is not dignified, but it might do. At any rate, you should try.'

'Fair philosopher, I will do as I am

bidden to the best of my ability. Have I received general orders, or will you condescend to details?'

'Make him publish something and take care that, whatever it is, it meets with the fate it deserves. You know best how, so no details.'

'By the way,' remarked St. John, 'anent reputation it is strange to consider how very short a time it lasts as compared with the period of its edification. Charles Martel lived a fairly long life, thought hard, worked hard, and fought hardest of all, yet ten lives later he was an impersonal name, and not much of that. That is to say, the greatest of men by slaving for one year secure a reputation for ten. It isn't worth the trouble.'

'Honour and Glory estimated on true mathematical principles by which it appears that $x + y$ is equal to z!' laughed Stella. 'I repeat it may do, in spite of all that. So go home at once and try. If you succeed, I shall be very much obliged to you.'

The above conversation bore fruit two months later in the publication of 'The Battle of the Books.' St. John had succeeded so far. He had managed Jonathan, the next thing to do was to manage the critics; but that in hands like his was no task. He was young, agreeable, rich, and had a fast growing reputation as one of the best speakers in the House of Commons, and therefore of course he had many friends, and into the hands of those among them who could appreciate it he put the 'Battle.'

The fashion was set forthwith, Jonathan's name was made, and the professional vituperators hissed in vain. The literary world bowed down and worshipped. Recognition had come at last. Well-merited success had dawned at the eleventh hour. Applications for the next work, no matter what he should write, poured in from the booksellers. Finance was no longer at dead low water level. The 'Battle' paid financially as well as otherwise. Callers at Moor Park began to ask for Mr. Swift, and Stella's remedy, in short, had a fair trial.

After letting well alone for a month or two, St. John indulged himself in a trip to see how the charm was working—so he wrote to Stella, in the first letter she had ever had from him—and for other reasons of more immediate moment, which had better perhaps be recounted in the next chapter.

CHAPTER XXI.

ON the day of this visit, Jonathan walked over in the morning to discharge a promise he had given Mrs. Dingley that no period of more than a week should elapse without the fate of the 'Tale' being duly notified to Manor Cottage. Success had raised his spirits, and his step, for the first time for years, had something of its old buoyancy. No wonder. To one so friendless and alone as was he, even the companionship of notoriety was something. So the worn, weary look on his ugly, fascinating face was less pronounced than usual, and, though the load at his heart was unlightened, still the stimulus of the moment made him bear it more easily than was his wont.

And certainly there was nothing at Manor Cottage calculated to depress him. Mrs. Dingley was all smiles and good wishes, while Stella, poor child, afraid perhaps of appearing too glad of the good news, was a little more demure than usual, and seemed in consequence to be all the more in earnest when she added her congratulations to those of her friend. If it make a woman demure to receive a proposal of marriage, that too may have had something to do with her manner; for that morning, not two hours before, Mr. Sawder's dapper groom had left at Manor Cottage a letter which invited her to do herself the honour of becoming Mrs. Sawder. This is by the way, however.

'Upon my word, Mr. Swift,' laughed

Mrs. Dingley, 'I never for a moment anticipated seeing you again. Last week's report put you beyond the serene atmosphere of Manor Cottage—away up out of sight in the empyrean in the—help, Stella, what is higher?'

'The seventh heaven.'

'That is here,' said Jonathan, gallantly.

'Nay,' persisted Mrs. Dingley, 'I am not complimenting you—quite the reverse; so spare your pretty speeches. I am asserting that I fully expect you to cut all your old friends, now my lords this and that ask you to dinner, and the Duke of Lionshire plays you as a trump-card.'

'Which you do solemnly affirm and declare upon your faith as a follower of Confucius?'

'Certainly, and ever so much more, too.'

'Then that faith aforesaid ought to take a place as a light porter. It bears up well under difficulties.'

'Well, we shall see,' persisted Mrs. Dingley, ' or rather we shan't—not you. A name in a news letter, a memory, a shadow of the past, and so on——'

'I appeal, Miss Johnson, is it fair to call me names, and such names, and to send them into the middle of time to come to lie in wait for me when I get there? And isn't it specially hard on a presumably original author to call him a shadow of the past?'

'It is a fine day," irrelevantly answered Stella.

'Worse and worse,' groaned Jonathan. 'What a broad hint to go out and try; and, joking apart, that is precisely what I must do, being miserably busy.'

'Nonsense,' protested the ladies; but Jonathan gave details of the arduous labours awaiting him which fully bore out his case.

'At any rate,' asked Stella, 'you can stay ten minutes until I can finish a letter I have got half written in the next room. I want you to deliver it for me,' and off she ran.

'Now,' said Mrs. Dingley, 'guess what news?'

'Miss Johnson has just left the room, is the latest.'

'No, no; seriously.'

'I don't know.'

'Then,' said Mrs. Dingley, 'prepare to be astonished. Mr. Sawder this morning asked Stella to marry him!—there!'

Mrs. Dingley was perfectly satisfied with the amount and nature of the astonishment Jonathan evinced. He leant back in his chair as though thunderstruck, and turned pale.

'Stella refused him,' hastily added the good-natured and very womanly woman, mistaking the reason which inspired such an excess of blank amazement. 'She refused him at once.'

'Ah, indeed,' remarked Jonathan, in an absent way. 'Ah, indeed;' and it was the only acknowledgment he vouchsafed for this last piece of reassuring information.

The fact was that the consideration of how Mr. Sawder's hints to himself could be reconciled with his proposing to Stella, fairly made his head reel with hopes and fears. He was hardly himself again when, five minutes after, Stella came back with two letters in her hand.

'I have let the cat out of the bag,' cried the elder lady.

'And I congratulate you, I'm sure,' said our hero, with a faint tremor in his voice. 'Is this the letter? Thank you. Good-bye. I must really be off;' and, taking the letter the blushing girl handed him, he was gone in a twinkling.

The ladies watched him from the window till he disappeared down the long, straight road, and then Mrs. Dingley, turning to her friend, said, from the abundance of her heart,

'Stella, that man *loves* you!'

And Stella thereupon laid her head on the other's shoulder and began to cry.

Let us leave her so, gentle reader, a few minutes, and go with Jonathan. He broke into a sling trot, as was very often his custom when excited, mechanically putting the letter in his pocket as he prepared to do so, and ensuring thereby that that letter should *not* be delivered according to the intention of the sender. Presently he reached Moor Park, his mind full of the strange news, and, once there, he found St. John waiting for him. The fate of the letter was sealed forthwith.

'Well, illustrious denizen of this dreary Dutch Paradise,' cried St. John, making a profound mock reverence, 'imagine that I am the bookseller, add a right angle to this my bow, and then you have a graphic representation of his respect and esteem for you, and of mine too, old fellow, joking apart !'

'Thank you,' said Jonathan. 'I owe it all to you, and can never be quits with you, never. Do you know, St. John, I believe a few years of this would waken me to life again. Not the life I might have lived if—you understand—but a life real, at any rate, as far as it goes, and infinitely better than the living death of the last few years. It is something to owe *that* to anyone, isn't it ?'

'If you bet upon any such wild opinions, all the editions in Christendom won't save you from ruin,' laughed St. John. 'It is wonderful how occasions for doing a fellow a good turn do crop up. Heaven only knows what you mightn't save me from in the next half **hour**. No, no, we may very easily be **quits yet for any** little **service I** have done you. We shall see. **Well, Sir** William is better, I hear.'

A shake of the head was the **answer.** Indeed Sir William was **very far from** being better; he was gradually, **slowly,** but surely, sinking.

'How **sad,' went on** St. John. 'In many ways **he** has been a very fine specimen of what an English gentleman ought to be. He gained a reputation for good **character** before **he** got one for talents, **and** that is the **right end** to begin **with.** It is **certainly** exceedingly degrading **to** a **man** like Somers to have such a bad moral character.'

This subject **of** conversation was evidently not, in its particular form, one to Jonathan's taste, so he widened it with one **of** those pithy aphorisms which were always at his command.

'Public life is private life,' he said.

'Hear, hear,' said St. John, 'there is no hanging a spare nature on a peg with one's great-coat, to be worn out of doors only. The men who pass a measure of spoliation are the men who, if necessary and convenient, would individually pick pockets.'

'Exactly. Henry VIII., had he been an apprentice instead of a prince, would have instinctively robbed a monastery.'

'The only difference was the consequent hanging.'

'Yes, and more's the pity.'

'So say I.'

'Nem. con., by Gad.'

'That being the case, it is time to change the subject,' remarked St. John ; 'by the way, our common friend Prior is desperately in love. His muse is plodding laboriously along through such a perfect crowd of Venuses, Cupids, trembling rays, cold effulgence, &c., &c., that upon my

honour the hustling and **pushing** of god-
desses and their attributes have fairly
by this time shouldered her out of joint.'

'Poor Prior,' said Jonathan, with a sigh,
'what a mercy it is, since **he** appreciates
adoring somebody, that he falls in love at
first sight. You see he has more chance
at first sight than **any other** time.'

'Swift, that is an unfounded slander.'

'St. John, no, it isn't.'

'What? You actually mean to say that
the more one sees **of a** woman the less
one will probably reverence, admire, love
her.'

'I never "mean to say." I hate the
very words, " mean to say ;" **but if it is not**
so I *know* that the **more one** reverences,
admires, and **loves** a woman, the less from
choice does one **see of** her—or else hus-
bands are the most self-sacrificing of men.'

St. John thought he saw an opening for
breaking his bad news gently to his friend,

for bad news he very well knew it would be to him.

'I am in love myself,' he said.

Jonathan did not move a muscle. He would not trust himself to speak. Was the great trial he had dreaded coming upon him?

'Evidently you don't believe me,' went on St. John, 'but for a wonder I am perfectly serious. There is no escape for me. I am desperately in love! What is more, from a silly pride I have struggled very hard to emancipate myself from my delicious bondage. The result of my kicking against the pricks is apparent—unconditional surrender, love first and pride nowhere.'

Still there was no reply. Jonathan was sitting quite still, and no change in his countenance betrayed his emotion. He felt what was coming. His apparent coolness deceived his friend.

'Perhaps the **poor** fellow won't mind much, after **all,** though **I** should succeed in cutting him out,' he thought.

'**You know very** well what my feelings towards *you* are, friend Jonathan. I trust that **our mutual** friendship will **be a** pleasure and profit to both of us as **long** as the petitioners will pray.'

Jonathan's lips moved in audible acknowledgment. In his **soul he was** cursing the day which made this man his friend, and which laid **him** under an obligation so deep that he was **obliged** to repay it, **cost** him what it might.

'**Yet amigo mio,**' pursued St. John, throwing in the Spanish **by way of** diversion. '**You will not wonder** if all my numerous visits **to** Moor Park—and they were pretty frequent during your absence —were not exclusively on your account. **Now** can **you** guess?'

'Go on.'

The tone made St. John start; it reminded him of a shipwreck he had once been in and the tone in which the captain had said, 'There is no hope; we are sinking.'

'Well, if you prefer not to risk your reputation for foreknowledge, would it surprise you if I should have fixed my affections on the Brown Beauty—if I should marry Hestor Johnson?'

It had come now, the ghastly duty faced him of saving his friend at the cost of blasting the character of this girl whom he loved, God knows how passionately; and Jonathan, in his anguish, wailed out,

'Stop, stop, for God's sake spare me. I loved her too—I love her more than you do. Say you will not marry her, swear it —I will swear it too, and I will never, never, never have another friend.'

He had risen, and was standing with his hands clenched, and the perspiration in great beads was upon his forehead. St. John was sincerely sorry, and somewhat amazed. He did not understand.

'Nay, Swift, I have not won her yet. She may refuse me,' he said, kindly. 'Sit down, man, don't look like that; be braver, Jonathan, for shame.'

'St. John, *you shall not ask her!*'

He was gasping for breath. The veins on his forehead stood out as though about to burst. His whole frame was trembling with emotion. And yet his voice was clear; commanding rather than entreating when he said, 'You *shall* not.'

'And what shall prevent me?'

'Your honour.'

'Come, come, old fellow,' said St. John, 'I am sorry to be your rival, but your rival I am. Of course Hestor is beneath me in social rank. All that I have considered. Honour falsely so-called shall not keep us apart—not for a moment. I shall go this instant to my fate,' and, suiting the action to the word, he rose, and was turning towards the door, but stopped. Jonathan's expression awed him; he never forgot it to his dying day.

A momentary pause, and then the gaunt secretary strode across the room, placed his hand lightly on the other's breast, and, looking with unutterable eyes straight into his, said, with awful calmness,

'I will save you, I must save you, St. John! The old man dying upstairs—Stella!'

There was no mistaking his meaning now; St. John too changed colour, and, turning on his heel, left the room without a word.

Where did he go? Straight upstairs to the bed of the dying statesman! He did not love, though he thought he did. It was love's twin brother, selfishness, that inspired him as it does the vast majority of so-called 'affection,' and so the risk of spreading groundless imputations about the character of this innocent girl never occurred to him. His only idea was to set his mind at rest one way or other. Meanwhile Jonathan stood just where St. John had left him, thinking, as in a kind of stupor, of the times long ago, *and looking into the mirror.*

Stop, Stella, stop, turn back again or stay for five short minutes before you enter that fatal room—alas! too late. Breathless with hurrying, lest the letter wrongly given should reach its destination through Jonathan's hands, Stella crosses the threshold, runs along the corridor, reaches the secretary's office, and knocks. No answer— Lauriel years ago had got no answer. She knocks again, then timidly opens the door, and sees—may the God to whose glory she has always striven to live be merciful to her! —that her lover is a jibbering maniac.

Her heart gives one wild, despairing leap,

and then seems to stop, but she makes a supreme effort to be calm for his sake. No one should see him thus but herself. No living soul; for it flashed across her that it would kill him to know, proud as he was of the mind God had given him, that he was *mad*, if by chance he should ever get better. So the brave girl stood watching, with the door just ajar, ready to slip away at the first sign of returning reason, and willing rather to see him die than call for help, which must betray him. And presently reason did come back, and Jonathan Swift, heart-broken, despairing, sank into a chair and buried his head in his hands. Then Stella quietly shut the door, and went swiftly home, and no one ever saw her smile again.

CHAPTER XXII.

INSTEAD of a note to the housekeeper at Moor Park, Jonathan had inadvertently taken the other letter, which Stella held in her hand, and that one was the reply to Mr. Sawder's proposal of marriage. To prevent the glaring impropriety of such a letter being delivered to the rejected suitor by one whom he probably recognised as a rival in his love, was why Stella paid her sadly-ending visit. But of course she had forgotten all about that now, and it was only when Mrs. Dingley ran out to meet her, and cried with comical despair, 'Well, I suppose too late. Mercury was too swift for you,' that this petty trifle, as it now seemed, re-appeared from beneath the shadow of the great trial that entombed it.

'I don't know. Mr. Swift was not in. I could not see him.'

It was the first story she had ever told in her life, and the secret must be kept. She dare not say she had forgotten.

'Ah!' replied Mrs. Dingley—'out! Well, I am sure he was not going to look at that letter again till he got home, if then. It had obviously gone the way of a great many other letters, to a week's residence in dear queer Jonathan's coat pocket. Did you leave a note for him?'

'No.'

'And why not, sweet Miss Wisdom?'

'I did not think of it.'

'Not really!'

'Yes.'

'Well, never mind; I will walk down that way a little. If Mr. Swift finds it, remembers it, dances upon it, or whatever phrase best expresses more luck than good management in the matter, he will instantly do your bidding and run to the vicarage, in which case I shall intercept him. Mind, Mary'—the solitary Manor Cottage servant —'is out, so don't go to sleep (you look tired enough), or I shall have to stay out in the cold. Moreover, look after the silver.'

And then Mrs. Dingley strolled away down the road, and Stella went into the drawing-room, picked up a book, and began to read it. A merciful Providence has ordained it so that ninety-nine people out of a hundred will wonder that she did not go to her room and burst into passionate tears. That is to say, ninety-nine people out of a hundred have no conception what real sorrow means. Long may they continue in their blessed practical ignorance of the fact that tears are prompted by a longing for relief, and *that* hopeless sorrow can never long for.

So Stella sat quietly reading that sublime play, Suckling's ' Aglaura,' caring nothing, of course, what should come next, but still reading with intelligence, if without interest. About half an hour passed thus, and then a knock at the door roused her. Book in hand, she went to undo the latch. That it was not Mrs. Dingley never occurred to her.

You see, for the time she was crushed, just as one who has received a great physical shock is crushed, numbed, as it were, and immobile. Her mind for the time had lost its elasticity, and only worked on the subjects immediately before it. Even when she had opened the door and saw Henry St. John, it was with an effort that she realised the fact, and forced herself to assume the ordinary bearing of a hostess. The momentary pause gave a ground to St. John to say, mock aggrievedly,

'Please may I come in?'

'Oh, certainly,' Stella answered, but in a tone which one often hears in the replies of people to questions they have imperfectly heard.

'Where is Mrs. Dingley?' he asked, pushing the drawing-room door more widely open to let her pass.

'I beg your pardon.'

'Fancy not being able to open the door and speak plain at the same time,' he laughed; 'but no matter. I only asked where Mrs. Dingley was, and that I know already.'

'Indeed!'

'Yes, I do: it was no secret, was it?'

'No. Will you sit down?'

'Thank you, it is weather for sitting still. So close and oppressive, isn't it? Only the direct sense of duty and pleasure drags me out of my chair or off my sofa during such meteorological mistakes.'

'Is it warm? Yes, I forgot. Shall I open the window?'

'Oh, dear, no; pray don't trouble. Nothing of that sort makes the faintest difference to me. And more especially, Miss Johnson, when my mind, or more especially still when my heart is pre-occupied, I—nor anybody else for the matter of that—think twice about the temperature. Oh, dear me, what a horrible common-place! Forgive me, I am not myself to-day.'

'Why?' said Stella.

'*Cogito ergo sum,*' he answered, 'and to-day I am thinking more of others than myself, so I suppose I amn't.'

'Who?' said Stella.

St. John looked curiously at her. The words invited to a declaration, but that was evidently and obviously accidental. Stella was thinking little and caring less about the conversation, and her replies were prompted by an intuitive perception of the course involving **least** trouble. However, there could be **no** better opportunity, and Mrs. Dingley might return **at** any minute, **so** he answered, boldly,

' **You.**'

Poor Stella's half dizzy head refused **to** grasp the idea meant **to be conveyed by** that **accentuated and pleading ' You' just** at first; **so she put her hand wearily** to her forehead for **a** moment and **answered,**

' I beg your pardon.'

Now evidently nobody could repeat a monosyllabic **statement of** such intensity **without** making it ridiculous, **so St. John** rose from his chair as an alternative, walked **across the** room, **took** Hestor **Johnson's** hand **in his** and kissed it. She raised her eyes to **his** inquiringly, and then what **the** situation meant seemed to dawn upon her. **St. John** saw that, and even in that moment of suspense he could not help noticing further how perfectly unmoved **she was by**

the discovery. No warm blush rose on her cheek as she gently withdrew her hand from his and motioned him to be seated again. There was a quiet indifference about the whole thing which amazed him. Thinking over it afterwards, he felt convinced that, had he there and then resumed his seat as he was bid and changed the subject by remarking on the weather, Stella would have made an appropriate reply and have been no whit astonished. The immediate effect upon St. John, however, was very different. He was about to be rejected. He, the rising statesman, handsome, rich, good-natured, clever as he was, had failed to win the heart of this friendless girl. The fuel of his injured vanity fed the flame of his love into a consuming fire. He seized her hand again and held it fast.

'Miss Johnson, Hestor darling, I love you; I am here to-day to tell you so, and to ask you to be mine. Give me leave to hold this little hand of right. Give me leave to love and cherish you always, always, my love, my beautiful. Say that you are not altogether indifferent to me, that you love me just a little. Say you will try to love me more and more as we go through the world together. You will, my Beautiful, won't you? Tell me so, Hestor.'

Still no blush, no tremor. She looked quite steadily into his eyes, and answered his question as though it had been on an abstract point of art.

'Thank you. This is a great compliment from one in your position to one in mine. But I shall never marry. Pray do not think about it any more.'

'You are cruel,' he pleaded; 'don't send me away like this. Give me a little hope. You are not really in earnest, are you? Am I such a wretch that there is no possibility of your ever caring for me? Oh!

Hestor, Hestor, for mercy's sake do not wreck my life like this! Think what you are doing before you drive me to despair. On my knees I beseech you.'

'I am very sorry,' she answered, in the same tone of far-off quiet, as though she were looking down from some distant world on the woes of another race, 'I am very sorry indeed. It is very good of you to care about me so much, and it is very ungrateful of me not to love you in return.'

'Then you do not?—not ever so little?'

'No. You are kind and good; but I do not love you.'

His manner changed at once. There was a reality about what she said in the face of which persistence would have been a mockery. He felt it so, and, like a true gentleman, was careful not to pain her by urging an evidently useless suit. But the idea occurred to him that in all human probability the issue would not have been the

same had the field been all his **own. He
had a rival**—he knew that ; and **now** he
knew that he had a successful **rival. St.**
John made what he fancied at the time was
a supreme **effort of** self-sacrifice, though
afterwards **he** learnt **that it** had been an
easier ordeal than it seemed.

'**I have a** rival ?' **he said.**

Stella **turned very pale, and was** going
to answer, as girls thus **placed have** always
answered since ever **the** world **was, '** You
have no right **to ask,' when** he stopped her.

'**Nay, do not be angry** with **me. I daresay you** have chosen rightly. **You do not**
love me ? Well, I will **learn to bear it ;**
and meanwhile, Miss **Johnson, I will be, in**
spite **of you,'**—and he smiled bravely—'the
very best **friend you have. Good-bye,' and,
picking up his** hat, he **had** left her before
she was fairly aware.

Presently Mrs. Dingley came back, **bearing an astonishing** story **about having seen**

one of the most rising statesmen in England taking a short cut for Moor Park across hedges and ditches at the rate of ten miles an hour.

' Having first been here, I suppose ?' she added.

'Yes,' answered Stella, quietly. 'Mr. St. John asked me to marry him, and I said no.'

'And a very great compliment too, my love,' was the reply, 'to dear, queer Jonathan.'

END OF THE SECOND VOLUME.

LONDON: PRINTED BY DUNCAN MACDONALD, BLENHEIM HOUSE